FREEDOM

What dark secret did the Founding Fathers of America hide, and who will stop at nothing to uncover it?

Navy SEALs in-training, Dane Maddock and Bones Bonebrake can't be in the same room without trying to kill each other, but soon find themselves caught up in a race with a secret society to solve a mystery that dates back to the founding of America. Find out how it all began in the action-packed first Dane and Bones Origins novella... Freedom!

Praise for the
Dane Maddock Adventures

"Freedom rocks! David Wood and Sean Sweeney serve up a great story of how it all began. Dane and Bones are in perfect form as they unravel a devilishly clever historical mystery that traces back to the early days of the nation." — **Sean Ellis, author of** *Fortune Favors*

"David Wood has done it again. *Quest* takes you on an expedition that leads down a trail of adventure and thrills. David Wood has honed his craft and *Quest* is proof of his efforts!" **David L. Golemon, Author of** *Legacy* **and** *The Supernaturals*

"Ancient cave paintings? Cities of gold? Secret scrolls? Sign me up! A twisty tale of adventure and intrigue that never lets up and never lets go!" -- **Robert Masello, author of** *The Medusa Amulet*

"A non-stop thrill ride triple threat- smart, funny and mysterious!" **Jeremy Robinson, author of** *Instinct* **and** *Threshold*

"Let there be no confusion: David Wood is the next Clive Cussler. Once you start reading, you won't be able to stop until the last mystery plays out in the final line." **Edward G. Talbot, author of** *2010: The Fifth World*

"An all-out blitzkrieg of a globe-trotting mystery-adventure that breaks from the action just long enough for a couple of laughs." **Rick Chesler, author of** *kiDNApped* **and** *Wired Kingdom*

"David Wood delivers again in Buccaneer with a fast-paced romp, complete with sunken treasure maps, hidden Templar churches and a secret organization that wants to resurrect an ancient kingdom. Fantastic!" **-J.F.Penn, author of the ARKANE thrillers.**

"David Wood captures all the adventure, twists and surprises, camaraderie, and treasure you could hope for in an action series." **-Kane Gilmour, Author of** *Resurrect* **and co-author of** *Ragnarok*

FREEDOM

A Dane and Bones Origins Story

David Wood
and
Sean Sweeney

Gryphonwood

Gryphonwood Press
PO Box 28910, Santa Fe, NM 87592

FREEDOM- Copyright 2013 by David Wood

Published by Gryphonwood Press.
www.gryphonwoodpress.com

ISBN 13: 978-1-940095-01-1
ISBN 10: 1940095018

If you love Dane and Bones, this book is dedicated to you.

Foreword

Readers often tell me they'd love to know more about how Dane and Bones got their start. What were they like "back in the day?" Did they have adventures in the SEALs? And what about these characters from their past whose names we've heard, but we've never met? If you've ever asked any of those questions, here's your answer.

Within these pages, you'll learn how Dane and Bones became friends, you'll meet characters you've only heard of (or heard on the telephone... Hint! Hint!) and join them on their first mystery. As with any Dane Maddock adventure, there's a little history, a lot of action, and a generous dose of humor. And, as always, we've played with a few historical details for the sake of the story.

I hope you enjoy reading this story as much as we enjoyed writing it, and I look forward to delving deeper into our favorite characters' past in future novellas.

David

Books by David Wood

The Dane Maddock Adventures
Dourado
Cibola
Quest
Icefall
Buccaneer
Atlantis (forthcoming)

Dane and Bones Origins
Freedom (with Sean Sweeney)

Stand-Alone Works
Into the Woods (with David S. Wood)
Dark Rite (with Alan Baxter)
Callsign: Queen (with Jeremy Robinson)
The Zombie-Driven Life

The Dunn Kelly Mysteries (Young Adult)
You Suck
Bite Me (forthcoming)

Writing as David Debord
The Silver Serpent
Keeper of the Mists
The Gates of Iron (forthcoming)

Books by Sean Sweeney

The Agent Series
Model Agent
Rogue Agent
Double Agent
Federal Agent
Promises Given, Promises Kept (forthcoming)

The Alex Bourque Mysteries
Cold Altar
Voir Dire

The Obloeron Prequels
The Rise of the Dark Falcon
The Shadow Looms

Stand-Alone Works
Zombie Showdown
Royal Switch
Eminent Souls
Freedom (with David Wood)
Redeemed (forthcoming)

Writing as John Fitch V
The Obloeron Trilogy
A Galaxy At War
Turning Back the Clock

PROLOGUE

Boston, Massachusetts
July 3, 1791

"Tell me it is not true." Samuel Adams stood ramrod straight, staring at the closed door of his guest room.

"It is."

If Adams harbored any doubts about the gravity of the situation, Revere's wan face and trembling hands drove it home. The silversmith collapsed into a chair and buried his face in his hands. Adams drew up a chair opposite him.

"What happened?"

Revere spread his fingers and looked between them at Adams. "The carriage had just pulled up in front of your house. A shot rang out and he slumped forward. He never uttered a sound." He sat up and rested his hands in his lap. "They heard a second shot, but it must have missed. His guards chased after the assassin while we brought him inside."

Adams had heard the shots, but never dreamed what they meant. "Where was he hit?" Adams realized he was holding his breath while he awaited the reply.

"The base of his skull. It is a grievous wound."

Adams let his breath out all in a rush. A cold certainty filled him. "Is there any hope?"

Revere shook his head. "I don't think so. He was still talking as we carried him in, but I've never seen anyone survive such a wound."

"What shall we do? Our union is weak. This could shatter us."

Revere raised his palms in a gesture of defeat.

They waited in silence for the physician. There was so much Adams wanted to say, but the words would not come. Finally, John Hart stepped out of the room and closed the door gently behind him.

A highly respected surgeon who had served admirably in the Revolution, there was no one Adams trusted more in this situation. Hart began to speak, but choked on his works. Adams and Revere looked away to permit him a moment to compose himself.

"I have done what I can for him," Hart finally managed.

"And?" Adams already knew what Hart's reply would be, but he felt compelled to ask.

"I fear he will not last the night."

Adams kept an iron grip on his emotions. There would be time later to grieve. Right now, he needed full command of his faculties. He turned to Revere. "Gather the others. The old meeting place at midnight."

Revere, rendered mute by despair, clasped hands with Hart and Adams, and hastily departed.

"You may see him if you wish." Hart sounded exhausted, or perhaps it was despair that rendered his voice weak as a newborn babe's. "He is awake, though I'm not certain he is aware of his surroundings."

"Thank you, doctor."

Adams saw Hart to the door, then returned to the sick room. He paused, his hand hovering above the doorknob, and steeled himself. Of all the trials he had faced for the cause of freedom, nothing had prepared him for this.

"May God help us," he whispered. His hand shaking, he opened the door and stepped inside.

CHAPTER 1

Dane Maddock looked up from his copy of *The Art of War* as the barracks door banged open and a voice boomed.

"Oh, yeah! BUDS is over, buddies!" Uriah Bonebrake, a six and-a-half foot tall Cherokee with a personality like fingers on a chalkboard, raised his fists in triumph. "Next stop, SQTs!"

"Don't forget jump school," Willis Sanders called down from his upper bunk.

"Child's play. I've been jumping off crap since I was a baby." Bonebrake high-fived Willis and turned to address the room at large. "Tonight, I'm gonna take five hundred dollars out of my account and hit the town. I'll spend half of it on cheap beer and loose women, and the other half I'll just waste. Who's with me?"

Dane muffled a fake cough as ragged cheers arose from the exhausted survivors of Basic Underwater Demolition/SEAL training. The candidates had completed eight weeks of Special Warfare Preparatory School, and a grueling six months of SEAL training. The past three-plus weeks had been spent on San Clemente Island, with Dane and his comrades put through grueling exercises designed to replicate days spent in action on the field of battle. How Bonebrake still had the energy to party was anyone's guess.

"I think Pope Maddock is judging me again. You have something you want to say, Your Holiness?"

"Would it matter if I did, Bonebrake?" Dane didn't bother to look up from his book. They'd had this conversation before, and he always found it a waste of time. Bonebrake was a clown destined for failure. Dane was amazed the man had made it this far.

"You think if I put termites in your skivvies they'd eat that stick that's up your butt?"

Dane sprang to his feet and squared off with the taller man. Bonebrake had six inches and twenty pounds on him, but Dane knew how to handle himself and, if truth be told, he'd been itching for a fight since day one of training.

"What the hell is your problem, Bonebrake? Why can't you, even once, conduct yourself with some decorum?"

"Big word from a little man. That's another reason nobody likes you. You're all superior."

"Come on, Bones," Willis said. "Don't be like that."

"Am I lying? Show of hands. Who here is Maddock's friend? Hell, who knows where he's from or what he does for fun when he's not strutting around with *proper decorum.*"

"We don't *not* like him," Pete Chapman, a lanky, sandy-haired man who'd earned the nickname "Professor" for his vast knowledge of useless trivia, called out. "He just does his thing." Chapman looked like he wanted to say more, but couldn't think of anything else to say.

Dane's cheeks burned. He took his training seriously, and he wasn't about to waste it goofing around with Bonebrake and his crowd.

"You're a joke, Bonebrake, and I'm going to laugh when you finally wash out."

"I'm going to earn the trident, and when I do, I'll have it tattooed on my ass so I can moon you every day." Bonebrake took a step closer, so they were almost touching. "And I've told before, call me Bones." He tried to poke Dane in the chest, but Dane slapped his hand aside.

Dane wasn't sure who threw the first punch, but suddenly he and Bonebrake were in the midst of an old-fashioned brawl. Bonebrake caught him over the ear with a right cross, which Dane answered with an uppercut, then bounced a jab off the big Indian's chin. Bonebrake didn't as much as wince. He grabbed Dane in a clinch, drove a knee into his rib cage, and head-butted him across the bridge of the nose.

Ignoring the pain, Dane broke the clinch and landed a solid roundhouse to the side of Bonebrake's knee. The bigger man wobbled and Dane leapt atop him. He managed to land a couple of solid elbow strikes before strong hands yanked them apart.

"Y'all done lost your minds!" Willis was the only man big enough to hold Bonebrake back on his own and, right now, it was all he could to keep him in check. "We're supposed to be brothers."

"Not a chance in hell," Bonebrake spat.

"Fine with me," Dane rasped through the Professor's choke hold.

"Maddock! Bonebrake!"

The sharp voice froze Dane's marrow and caused Bonebrake to immediately cease his struggles. Hartford Maxwell, or "Maxie," was their commander and a man for whom Dane had the utmost respect. Never before had he heard such anger in Maxie's voice. "My office in ten!"

"Yes sir!" both replied, but Maxie had already turned away from them. He strode out the door and closed it behind him with a bang.

Dane and Bonebrake exchanged looks of loathing, but otherwise ignored each other until they reached Maxie's office ten minutes later.

Maxie was on the telephone when they arrived. He waved them inside, and they stood at attention until he ended the call. The office, austere as Maxie himself, held only a matching gray metal desk and file cabinet, and a chair. A single pad of legal paper, an empty "In Box," a telephone, and a framed photograph of an attractive blonde girl of about sixteen sat atop his desk. When he finally hung up, he propped his feet up, laced his fingers behind his head as if he were lounging in a hammock, and regarded them with a steely gaze that matched the hair on his temples. He was solid in every way, and not a man to be trifled with.

After an uncomfortable silence, he let his breath out in a huff. "At ease."

Dane tried to relax his posture, but found himself

too tense to do anything but stare straight ahead. Bonebrake didn't seem to have that problem. He sidled over to Maxie's desk, picked up the photo, and whistled.

"Is this your daughter? Man, she is going to be a beauty. She must get her looks from your wife's side of the family, huh?"

Maxie sat up, relieved Bones of the photo, and replaced it on his desk. "That's my daughter Kaylin and, yes, she does take after her mother. A fate that hopefully awaits any children you might have." He laced his fingers together, rested them on the desk, and gave them another silent stare.

"I'm sorry..." Dane began.

"I don't want your apologies, Maddock. I want the two of you to change your behavior. You're two of the finest I've ever trained, and I don't want to lose either of you, but you pull a stunt like this again, I'll come down on you like Ric Flair. You get my meaning?"

"Yes, sir!" Bonebrake said. "My grandfather loved Flair."

Dane had no idea who Ric Flair was, but he got the gist. "Yes, sir."

"All right, Bonebrake. Tell me what you know about Maddock."

"What do you mean?" Bonebrake cocked his head like a confused puppy.

"I'm sorry. Was that question too difficult for you? Tell me about Maddock. And I don't mean what he looks like or what he eats for breakfast. What do you know about him as a man?"

"Not much. I just know he thinks he's better than everyone else. He doesn't respect or appreciate the rest of us."

Dane wanted to object, but held his tongue

Maxie turned to Dane. "Your turn. Tell me about Bonebrake."

"He doesn't take anything seriously. He wants respect, but he has no respect for anyone or anything."

Maxie sighed. "You morons do realize I could make your lives miserable if I wanted to?"

Dane and Bonebrake nodded.

"If you don't want that to happen, you're going to do something for me. Blow this chance, and the next time you step out of line your dreams of becoming a SEAL are over."

This time, their nods were reluctant.

"My family and I were supposed to take a little trip to Boston during leave time," Maxie continued, "but now her mother has decided to come for a visit." He rolled his eyes. "The tickets are non-refundable, so I've had two of them transferred into your names." Maxie tore the top sheet off his note pad and slid it across the desk. On it was an airline name, and dates and departure times for the outbound and return flights.

Dane's mouth went dry. "I'm afraid I don't understand."

"You two are going to take a trip to Boston. I happen to know that you like Colonial history and Bonebrake likes bars. You'll find plenty of both there. You'll be in the birthplace of the American Revolution on the Fourth of July. Maybe that will remind you two why you serve and who is and isn't your enemy."

"Maxie, you can't..." Bonebrake stammered.

"Do you really want to finish that sentence?"

Apparently, Bonebrake did not, because he lapsed into sullen silence.

"I expect you two to spend your leave together. Every minute of it. I'm going to interrogate you when you get back. Don't give me reason to believe you did anything other than spending time getting to know and respect one another. You leave tonight, so you'd better get packed. Now get out of my sight."

A million thoughts raced through Dane's head, but he voiced none of them. What would be the point? Leave time at close quarters with Bonebrake. He had to hand it to Maxie. The man knew how to dole out punishment.

CHAPTER 2

Even within the confines of the subway car, Dane covered his ears as the screech of steel wheels sent a shrieking tremor down his spine.

North Station, the screechy, tinny voice called out. *Exit on the right, please. Thanks for riding the T.*

The doors slid open. A wall of exhaust and thick, humid air hit him right in the face. Who would have thought Boston could make him miss the sweltering heat of South Florida?

"I really don't get why we're doing this." Dane grimaced and surveyed the scene. "I was all ready for a nice evening of resting up from the flight and doing absolutely nothing. But no, Bonebrake, you had to drag me out here."

"Relax, Maddock." Bones gave Dane's shoulder a friendly shake. "You're wound up tighter than my grandmother's girdle. Loosen up and get into the spirit of things. We're on leave, dude. Guys like us, we're supposed to have a few drinks, maybe get into a fight. You know, experience life."

They turned right and headed down the stairs to the turnstiles. Another passageway skewed off to their left, across Causeway Street. Several people walked that way, some wearing replica Red Sox jerseys. "Cheer up. You're going to get to study that Colonial History stuff that you like so much."

"I was going to do that... after I slept," Dane countered, "but somebody wouldn't shut up until I agreed to go drinking with him."

Bonebrake smirked as they passed through the turnstiles and headed down the long staircase and out to the street. Dane looked around and saw the filth that coated the once-green steel of the elevated subway station, as if exhaust fumes clung to the metal and constricted it, squeezing the life out of the neighborhood. They entered the converging shadows as they walked along the sidewalk adjacent to the decaying Boston Garden. Several of the street level store fronts were empty, the windows blackened. Dane wrinkled his nose at the acrid stench of stale urine.

"We've already learned one new thing about Boston." Bonebrake fanned the air in front of his nose. "It's apparently the world's biggest urinal."

Dane smirked. He refused to laugh at Bonebrake's wisecracks. He still couldn't believe Maxie had bullied them into this trip. Then again, Maxie was a good judge of character. If he saw something in Bonebrake, Dane knew he ought to give the guy a chance.

They walked a few more feet before Bonebrake guided him through an open door. "Now, this is my kind of place."

Dane grimaced. It was exactly what he'd envisioned, perhaps "feared" would be a better word, when Bonebrake suggested they go out for a few beers. It wasn't a high-class establishment where the wood had a high glossy shine on the bar, or well lit during the day to let potential customers know it was open to quench a hearty Bostonian thirst. Bonebrake had laid out their options for him: this place, or a bar in something called the Combat Zone. Dane had figured this to be the safer option. No telling what Bonebrake might get them into in a place with that name.

They sat down at the bar. Several televisions surrounded the perimeter, most tuned to pregame coverage of the Red Sox at Fenway Park. One had Keno playing, the timer ticking down to the next game. The place wasn't nearly half-full. A few men played pool in the corner, the crack of the stick against the ball rising above the blended sounds of conversation, laughter, and baseball talk. Outside and above, the sounds of another subway train rolled through the station. A motorist honked their horn.

"Nice ambience. It's like drinking in the middle of a traffic jam."

Bonebrake shook it off. "Relax, dude. You need a drink, and an hour with the skankiest chick I can hook you up with."

Dane winced. "Does your voice have a volume control?"

Bonebrake made a face as the bartender approached.

"What can I get you guys?"

Dane ordered a Dos Equis, which earned him a sneer from the bartender, while Bonebrake ordered a

Samuel Adams. The bartender proffered two bottles, one green and one brown. He removed the caps and passed them over on warped cardboard coasters. Dane paid and took a long drink, enjoying the rich flavor, the feel of the cool liquid sluicing down his throat, and the chilled bottle smooth in his hand.

"Thanks for the drink. Next round's on me." Bonebrake held up his bottle, "A toast to Maxie and the United States Navy. May they and all the babes we meet tonight regret our first leave as Navy SEALs."

"We're not all the way through training," Dane clinked his bottle against Bonebrake's.

"Yeah, but the hard part's over."

"You think so, do you?"

"Maddock, some guys see the glass as half-empty. You see it as half-empty and filled with poison. You know that?"

Dane made no reply. It wasn't the first time he'd been told he was a pessimist. They settled into an awkward silence and Dane tried to gather in the ambiance of the run-down sports bar, what little it had. Truth was, calling it a dive would be high praise. A few items of sports memorabilia hung on the once salmon-colored walls.

Dane wasn't a huge sports fan, but he recognized the teams and faces. Pictures of Bruins retired numbers superimposed on the black and yellow spoked B, while a large photo of Bobby Orr hanging in mid-air took up half of a wall. Images of Larry Bird, Bob Cousy, Bill Russell and Red Auerbach held up a Celtics-themed wall, while still more of Ted Williams, Carl Yastrzemski and a young Roger Clemens were behind the bar. A solo minuteman huddling over a football held a special place among the mementoes. Other than that, it was dark, dirty, and the clientele, if the patrons could call themselves that, wore tank tops and cut-off jean shorts, most favoring a few days' stubble.

Dane looked to Bonebrake. While he sported neither a dirty tank top, nor stubble running along his jawline, the tall Indian wore a garnet and black-colored South Carolina basketball jersey with the number 22 on the front, along with khaki shorts, bright red Converse high tops, and no socks. They cut an odd figure, Dane in a Hawaiian shirt and Nikes a few sizes smaller than his cohort's gunboats.

Dane absent-mindedly picked at the green label with his fingernail. He didn't know how this weekend would play out. He and Bonebrake drove each other nuts, though Dane felt he had reasons aplenty to dislike the man. Bonebrake was abrasive, obnoxious, and immature. On the positive side of the ledger, he had the mettle to complete the first stages of SEAL training. He finished pulling the label off and dropped it on the bar. Bonebrake laughed and flicked the label onto the floor.

"What's so funny?" Dane asked, turning to his partner.

"You, dude. You're so sexually frustrated. How many labels have you pulled off bottles of beer in the past two years?"

"Oh, come off it. I'm not sexually frustrated, Bonebrake."

"Hey, I told you. My name is Bones."

"Sorry." He paused. "What kind of name is Bones, anyway?"

"It's just a nickname I picked up when I was just a little redskin."

Dane blinked. Bones loved to make people uncomfortable by throwing around derogatory terms about his own heritage.

"Many moons ago, long before I first pulled handle on slot machine."

"Okay, I get it." Dane took another drink.

"No, I don't think you do, dude. You don't get me at all."

"What I get is that you don't have a serious," he paused and grimaced, "*bone* in your body."

Bones threw his head back and laughed. "You said *serious bone*. Sexually frustrated, just like I said. Speaking of which, I wonder if there are any ladies who might like to enjoy my..."

"That's what I mean. You think everything's a joke."

"And you don't know how to lighten up." Bones gestured with his bottle. "If you'd get over yourself, maybe some of your comrades in arms, other than yours truly, would warm up to you. Maybe a few girls, too."

"I don't know." Dane took another swig of beer, remembering what Bones had said to him the previous day. *That's why nobody likes you.* People respected him, he was sure of that. Maybe Bones was right. He didn't exactly have any close friends in the service. "I'm fine with the way things are."

"That's sad, bro. There's a lot more to life than following the rules."

Dane suppressed the sudden impulse to punch Bones, but he'd been there, done that, and it hadn't helped things. In fact, the fight seemed to make Bones like him even more. Now, he'd made it his personal mission to lighten Dane up, or at least convince him he was too rigid. He turned to stare at Bones, who stared out across the bar.

"That's not cool."

Dane followed Bones' gaze to the far corner of the bar, where two young women were trying to evade the attentions of an aggressive bar patron. Neither could have been more than twenty years old; probably college kids with fake IDs who were looking for adventure and got more than they bargained for.

"I think I've found my first fight of the evening." Bones cracked his knuckles and made to slip down off his bar stool.

"I got it." Dane set his shoulders and marched across the bar. He knew Bones was eager for a brawl, but he didn't want to spend the evening trying to bail a guy out of jail who wasn't even his friend, and he certainly didn't want to get locked up along with him. With Dane's luck, they'd probably wind up in the same cell. He imagined calling Maxie and telling him they'd been arrested. That would be fun.

The man had the two girls corralled in the corner, his hands pressed against the wall on either side of them.

"There you are." Dane shouldered the man aside without even looking at him and reached out to take the girls' hands. "Dad's been looking for you. We need to hit the road." Surprise and gratitude mingled on the girls' faces. And they followed Dane to the door. "I don't think this is the sort of place you two ought to be hanging around," he told them.

"Definitely not." The shorter of the two reached up and dragged a fingernail down his chest. "We're gonna find a club or something. Want to come with?"

Dane smiled. Her slender figure, glossy black hair and sparkling blue eyes held plenty of appeal, but she was a kid. "How old are you two, really?"

"Nineteen." The girl blushed and her friend giggled.

"You two have a good night and stay out of dives like this."

He returned to the bar to discover Bones had ordered up another round. "Thanks, man."

"No problem." Bones paused. "Tell me something, and I'm not trying to give you a hard time here, I really want to know. Why didn't you drop that guy?"

Dane sighed. "I wanted to, but I guess I'm always thinking a few steps ahead. I punch the guy, he calls the cops, I go to jail, maybe both of us if you mouth off, we have to call Maxie and it gets worse from there."

"That's why you take it outside. Insult his manhood, get him all riled up so he can't refuse, then you go out back where nobody can see, take him out quick, and run. He'll probably be too embarrassed to call the cops, nobody likes admitting he got his ass kicked, but even if he does, you've already found another bar long before they take the report. Besides, you're a stranger to him. Which is why I always pay with cash. Can't get my name off a credit card receipt that way."

"So you *do* think ahead."

"Sure. The difference between you and me is, you plan for the worst, I plan for the awesomest."

"That's not a word, you know."

"Seriously, Maddock, how many beers is it going to take for you to be... human?"

Dane found himself laughing. "Cheers, Bones." This time, when they clinked their bottles together, it didn't feel like compulsory behavior. "Speaking of not acting human, what is it with you and defaming your heritage?"

"Defaming?" Bones sat his bottle on the bar and furrowed his brow.

"Yeah. You're not really what I picture when I think of a Native American. You throw around words that others find offensive, like *redskin*."

"I love their football team! I've got two or three of their jerseys. Plus the Braves, Blackhawks, the Tarheels..."

"So, you're from North Carolina, you like teams with Native American mascots, yet you're wearing a South Carolina jersey?"

"Are you kidding? South Carolina are the 'Cocks. Those corn-fed South Carolina girls like those big old strong..."

"I get it, I get it."

"Seriously, though. I do like to shock people and piss them off a little." Bones paused, spinning the bottle in his hands. "But most folks are too uptight about the whole thing. They're all gung ho about political correctness, getting their loincloths in a twist. Yet here they are, opening casinos on tribal lands, trying to make a buck. They want people to think they worship the old gods and hold the old ways, but they worship the almighty dollar like the rest of us. They're so damn serious about getting offended-- they're like you, only with burnt umber skin."

Dane huffed his amusement. "You're a deeper thinker than I thought."

"Lower people's expectations and it's easier to take them by surprise."

They lapsed into companionable silence. Bones amused himself by whistling into the mouth of his empty bottle and looking around the bar. "Hey, Maddock. You remember the advice I gave you about taking it outside?"

"Sure."

"Good. You're going to need it, because it looks like that dude finally got up the courage to make something of it."

CHAPTER 3

"I usually don't let anybody mess with me when I'm hooking up the ladies," a familiar voice called from somewhere behind them, "but I just couldn't get over my shock at seeing my buddy, little Jane Maddock again."

Dane paused and closed his eyes. It couldn't be. He stole a glance over his shoulder. "Oh, no way."

"You know him?" Bones asked.

"Unfortunately, yes. We were at Annapolis together."

Bones' eyebrows rose. "Oh ho, an Academy brat."

"Pretty much. Upperclassman by the name of Paccone. Marc Paccone."

"Does he like his martinis shaken instead of stirred?"

Dane shook his head. "He was a punk. Big and dumb. Loved to harass the underclassmen."

Bones nodded.

"Hey Maddock, I'm talking to you." The voice drew closer.

"He turned out to be a huge bully and a sadist, freaking out a lot of Midshipmen. Word was, he had a connection with a senator, an uncle or something, and he used that to keep people from reporting him."

"So he was a bully *and* a coward."

"Big time. Last I heard, he was assigned to Charlestown."

Bones blinked.

"Charlestown, as in right around the corner? On board the *USS Constitution*?"

"Yep."

"You would think a guy like that wouldn't get such an honor. I guess the senator hooked him up."

Dane stiffened as Paccone stepped up to the bar, ignoring Bones as if he were a cigar store Indian.

"You aren't going to say hello to your old friend, Maddock?"

"I always speak to old friends. Problem is, I don't see any in here." Dane turned and met the man's eye. He forced himself not to wince at Paccone's toxic breath. It smelled as if the bartender had mixed him a lethal combination of motor oil and Jose Cuervo.

"Come on. You steal my action and don't even say hello when we haven't seen each other in so long." Paccone grinned, the light gleaming off the damp sheen of sweat on his forehead.

"Not long enough, Paccone."

Paccone's eyes narrowed to slits. "What's that supposed to mean? We were best buds."

"In your soggiest dreams, maybe," Dane countered. Out of the corner of his eye, he saw Bones cover a laugh by coughing into his clenched fist.

Paccone's jaw worked and Dane could almost see

the gears in Paccone's mind turning at three-quarter speed. After a few seconds Paccone tensed up and clenched his fists. "Aw, are you still mad that I ragged on you a little? If it bothered you so much, why didn't you ever stand up to me, Jane?"

"How about," Bones interrupted, "you go sober up and get a freakin clue, dude? We're trying to enjoy our drinks, here."

Paccone paused and turned his attention to Bones, his eyes wide as if he had just discovered the big man's presence.

"And who the hell are you, peckerwood?"

"Dude, we've got to work on your slang. Peckerwood is for rednecks and white trash. You know, people like you."

"Whatever. Why don't you keep your big nose out of my business? I think Jane Maddock has a problem with me, but he's not man enough to do anything about it."

"Hey," the bartender called, "we're not going to have any brawling in here, you got that?"

"Definitely not," Dane said. "We were just about to step outside." He'd had enough of Paccone, and it was high time he did something about the years of resentment that festered inside him. He tossed a ten on the bar and motioned for Paccone to lead the way.

"Ladies first." Paccone made a mocking bow and gestured toward the door.

Dane smiled and led the way out onto the street without another word. They melded into the shadows of one of the side streets, well out of sight of any passers-by.

"Tell your friend here not to jump in." Paccone rolled up his sleeves and scowled at Bones.

"He won't." Dane knew he should be worried about someone calling the cops, or Paccone using his senator connection to screw up Dane's chances with the SEALS, but he found himself feeling surprisingly relaxed. Apparently, Bones was rubbing off on him, and even that didn't seem to worry him. He raised his fists, turned slightly, and rose up on the balls of his feet, ready to spring.

Paccone charged in, swinging a wild haymaker that Dane easily ducked. He drove a punch into Paccone's gut. The man had gone soft around the middle, and he grunted as the breath left him in a rush. He reeled backward, Dane following, peppering him with crisp jabs. Paccone backed into a dumpster, bounced off, and charged forward, his face a mask of crimson from cuts above both eyes and a bloody nose. He tried to grapple with Dane, but Dane grabbed him by the ears, yanked his head down, and drove his knee up into Paccone's face. Paccone's knees gave out and he dropped to all fours. A knee to the temple and he was flat on his face.

"Okay, so I took it outside. What's the next step?" Dane asked.

"Run like hell!"

They dashed down the darkened street, slowing only when they were back on the main drag. No sense in drawing unnecessary attention. Bones got enough of that for being a six and-a-half foot tall Cherokee with a weightlifter's build.

"Nice job, Maddock. Good thing *our* fight got broken up as soon as it started. I wouldn't want you messing up my pretty face."

"I didn't need you beating me to a pulp either. I'm ugly enough as it is."

"True." Bones made a solemn nod. "You know, the best part of our evening is, we can cross two things off our leave bucket list: drinking beer and getting into a fight."

Dane glanced up as another subway train passed overhead, the sound of steel wheels rocking away. "Yes, but what else can we do that won't have us thrown into the back of a paddywagon?"

Bones opened his mouth, but froze at the sound of screeching tires, the sick thunk of bone against sheet metal, and shattering glass.

Both men turned their heads to see one of Boston's famed yellow taxis stopped in the middle of the street with an uncharacteristic human hood ornament lodged in its windshield.

"Oh, crap!" Dane dashed toward the scene of the accident with Bones right behind him.

By the time they reached the cab, traffic had ground to a halt. The cab driver, a heavy set Hispanic man, stood outside the driver's side door, a look of disbelief plastered across his tanned face. Another motorist stood outside his car, a bulky Motorola cell phone pressed to his ear, presumably calling emergency services to the scene.

The injured man had managed to roll off the hood

of the cab and now lay on his back in the middle of the street. His lined face and silver-sprinkled brown hair put him at about sixty years old, give or take a few. He wore a tweed coat with worn elbow patches, much like a college professor would wear.

Dane knelt and pressed his fingers against the man's carotid artery. His pulse throbbed madly, as if he had just run a marathon, and then suddenly weakened.

He isn't going to make it, Dane thought, as the whine of sirens pierced the air. "Hold on. The paramedics are on the way."

"Hey, what are you doing to that guy?" the cabbie demanded.

"Stand back, sir." Bones grabbed the protesting taxi driver and pulling him away. "We're trained in first aid."

"Never... mind... the para.. medics." The man's blue eyes were glassy and his chest labored as his lungs fought to take in precious air. "Promise me..." he rasped, foamy blood bubbling from the corners of his mouth. He grabbed the front of Dane's shirt with surprising strength. "Promise..."

Dane didn't know this man from Adam, but he found himself nodding. How could he deny the request of a dying man? "Of course, anything." He didn't know why he had said it but, at his words, the man smiled.

"Thank you," he wheezed. "You must... find... the lantern. The lantern... is the key... to everything."

"Lantern?" Dane didn't understand.

The man reached into his coat pocket, wincing with the effort, and pulled out a cream-colored rectangle. "This... is the name of... a colleague." He pressed the square into Dane's hand. "Was expecting me. Must find it... Open the gates of freedom."

"What do you mean?"

The man's eyes glazed over and he seemed to be drifting out of consciousness.

"Sir?"

"The British... are... coming." With that odd declaration, he fell silent, and breathed no more.

Dane stood and backed away. A crowd had gathered around, and he worked his way through the throng to where he saw Bones' head sticking up over the others. Bones raised an eyebrow when he saw what Dane held: a small business card. He held it out for Bones to see.

Beneath the dead man's bloody thumbprint, the card read: *Prof. Gregory Remillard, American History, Boston University.*

Dane took a deep breath and slipped the card into his pocket as soon the sirens drew closer. A police cruiser arrived a few seconds later.

An officer climbed out and approached the cab driver. A few minutes later, he approached Dane and Bones.

"I'm officer MacDougal." Dane and Bones gave their names and MacDougal nodded. "You gave him first aid?" he asked.

"We would have," Dane said, "but his injuries seemed to be internal. We just stayed with him until he died."

"Cabbie says the guy just ran right out in front of

his cab. Any idea why?"

Dane shook his head. "We heard the accident, but didn't see it."

Just then, a second patrol car came to a screeching halt alongside MacDougal's car. A thickset blond man piled out and stalked over to where they stood. His nameplate read "O'Meara."

"I got this, MacDougal."

"Quick response time, Lieutenant." Something about MacDougal's tone gave Dane pause. "I'm surprised to see you out here."

"It's your lucky day. I just happened to be in the area when I heard the call. I'll take over from here."

"I can take their statements. No need for you to waste your time."

"It's all right." O'Meara's smile revealed coffee-stained teeth. "I like to do some real police work here and there. You can get back on patrol. It's not like we've got a shortage of crime in the city."

MacDougal seemed reluctant, but he finally gave a single nod and headed back to his vehicle.

In an instant, O'Meara's genial tone turned serious.

"What happened here?"

"We're not sure. The cabbie said the old man ran out in front of him. We got here too late to help."

"Did the victim say anything to you? I mean, did he tell you why he ran out into the road like that?"

Dane looked to Bones for half a second before he returned his gaze to O'Meara. "I think he might have been having a mental breakdown or something. All he said was, 'The British are coming.'"

The officer barked a laugh. "Perfect. Probably thought he had to get to the Old North Church in a hurry. "You gave your names to MacDougal?" Dane and Bones said they had. O'Meara told them they were free to go, turned on his heel, and headed over to speak to the cabbie.

Bones sidled up to Dane. "That's not all the old dude said. I can tell by the look in your eye," he whispered. "You just lied to a cop."

Dane didn't smirk or show any indication that his face held any emotion. He pocketed the officer's business card along with the one the dying man had given him. "Surprised?"

"Just a little bit. But I'm proud of you. I might turn you into a normal human being yet."

"He said," Dane continued, watching as O'Meara stood by the body, "something about finding a lantern." He paused and swallowed. "I have no idea what he means, but he gave me the name of someone to contact. He might have been crazy, but he made me promise I'd find this lantern for him."

"Let me guess, you've got some weird family slogan, like, *A Maddock always keeps his promises.*"

Dane motioned for Bones to follow him further away from the scene and the possible prying ears of the Boston Police. "Not exactly a slogan, but I do try to keep my word." Their footsteps clopped on the asphalt until they reached the stairs leading back to the subway.

"It's cool with me if you want to follow up on this. I'm kind of curious about the whole thing. The dude might have been out of his mind from shock, but maybe not. What do you want to do about it?"

"I think I'd like to scratch that Colonial American History tour off the on-leave bucket list." Dane took the stairs two at a time. "Something more interesting has just come up."

CHAPTER 4

"Where are all the hot chicks?" Bones put his hands on his hips and scowled.

"It's Boston University in the middle of summer semester. It's not like the place is bustling with coeds right about now."

"That's the only thing I liked about college."

"You went to college?" Dane immediately regretted the question. He didn't think Bones was stupid, just annoying.

"I got a two-year degree. That's all I could stand. The classroom isn't for me, bro."

They crossed Commonwealth Avenue at a trot and entered a tan, sandstone building. The sign on the door read, Warren Towers. The moment they stepped inside. Dane tugged at his damp collar and shivered as a wave of cool air engulfed him.

"Where do you think we'll find this professor?"

"Good question. I'm hoping that someone in one of these offices can point us in the right direction. I'd rather take the time to ask around than wander aimlessly from building to building, not knowing where we're going."

"Bet you he's on vacation. Why would you stay on campus when all the babes are gone and there's no classes to teach? I'd be on a beach somewhere, partying."

"I'm sure they have summer courses, just not as many as during the regular school year."

"You sure you don't want to call? His number's on the card."

"Not if we don't have to. Our reason for visiting is weird enough as it is, and if the guy who gave us this card is a friend, that's the sort of news that ought to be delivered in person.

"Okay, I got this. What's the professor's name again? Remillard?" Bones disappeared into an office and came out a few minutes later, with directions, plus a name and phone number.

"We already know his name and number. Why did you get it again?" Dane asked.

"What are you talking about? I got the secretary's number. She wasn't bad looking." They stepped out into the summer heat and Bones shifted his leather jacket. "Actually, she wasn't all that hot, but she had big hair. You know what they say about big-haired women."

"No, and I don't think I want to."

They wandered along Commonwealth Avenue, taking in the sights, and Dane felt that he hadn't entirely missed out on his Colonial sightseeing. They arrived at a five-story sandstone building with bow front columns, and the similar buildings on either side gave the impression of vertical rolling hills. Dane remembered reading that this style of architecture had been popular in the mid-1800s and had extended from Beacon Hill down to the brownstones of the Back Bay.

A red brick walkway bisected well-manicured green lawns, and climbed the three stairs up to a heavy wood and glass door. Bones open the door and waved Dane through. They found Remillard's name and office number on a faculty directory posted on the wall.

"Second-floor." Dane pointed to Remillard's name. "Let's go."

The clacking of a manual typewriter guided them down the hall to an open door. Dane knocked twice and stepped inside. A middle-aged woman with white, permed hair, a flowery blouse, and enough extra pounds to give her the appearance of lumpy dough, looked up and smiled.

"Can I help you?" The woman's gravelly voice put her at about two packs a day, if Dane did not miss his guess.

"Yes, we are here to see professor Remillard."

"Do you have an appointment?" The woman scowled at Bones in his ripped jeans and leather jacket.

"Not exactly," Dane replied. "We are acquaintances of a colleague of his."

"Which colleague?"

Dane hesitated. They had hit a wall of flesh, polyester, and hairspray. "Well, you see, the man didn't actually say…"

"I'm not busy, Margaret. If I have visitors, send them in," a voice called from the adjoining room.

Margaret shot an angry look at them and inclined

her head toward a door to their right.

"We appreciate the help." Bones smiled and winked at Margaret, who actually blushed. From the look in her eyes, Dane wouldn't have been surprised if she giggled like a schoolgirl.

Professor Remillard, a tall, rail-thin man with salt-and-pepper hair and a silver-washed goatee, wore a red golf shirt, tan khaki pants, and little, round glasses that hung precariously on the tip of his thin nose. He welcomed them into an office stuffed with old, leather bound books on sagging shelves. The heavy scent of old paper permeated the air, reminding Dane of Fifteenth Street Books in Coral Gables, Florida, a favorite hangout in his early teen years. An IBM computer sat on one end of the professor's cherry lacquered desk, and a tweed coat boasting the same elbow patches that the deceased man's coat displayed, hung on the back of an office chair.

"Thank you for seeing us without an appointment, professor." Dane hoped the man wouldn't kick them out as quickly as he'd welcomed them.

"It's all right." Remillard waved the thanks aside. "It's summer time, my course load is light, and there aren't many students around who need help with their schedules for next semester." He sat down and looked at them with interest. "How may I help you?"

"One of your colleagues gave us this." Dane handed him the card.

Remillard saw the bloody thumbprint and frowned. "Who gave this to you?" Dane gave a brief description of the deceased, and Remillard nodded.

"That sounds like Nick Andrews. He was supposed to meet me last night, but he never showed. Is something wrong?"

Dane thought it best to start at the beginning, so he first broke the news of the accident. Remillard's eyes misted, and he invited them to take a seat, his voice hoarse with grief. Dane and Bones settled into matching, straight-backed wooden chairs, and Dane continued his story.

"He made me promise to find the lantern," Dane finished lamely.

"Did he say anything else?"

"The British are coming." Bones raised an eyebrow. "We figure he might have been losing it at the end, you know, from the shock of the accident."

Remillard fixed them with an appraising look, as if he could and read their intentions. Leaning back and folding his arms across his chest, he took a deep breath and exhaled slowly.

"Can I trust you gentlemen?" he asked, and then chuckled. "A foolish question, I know. An untrustworthy man would, by his very nature, assure me he could be trusted."

"We're Navy," Bones answered, as if that were enough.

"In the SEAL program," Dane added.

Remillard's face crinkled in a wry smile. "I don't suppose it matters. Nick put his trust in you, and it's not my place to countermand his wishes. Besides, you know enough that you could easily find out the rest if you wanted to." He cleared his throat, sat up straight, and rested his palms on the desktop. "How much do you know about Paul Revere?"

"I know he was a silversmith. And, of course, I know about the Midnight Ride."

"One if by land, two if by sea," Bones added.

"That's it exactly."

"You mean he was talking about the lantern from the Old North Church?" Dane shifted in his chair.

"The very one."

"Seriously? I was just being a smartass."

"But there were two lanterns. Like Bones said, one if by land, two if by sea."

"Three if the British called in an airstrike," Bones added.

Dane closed his eyes and pressed his hands to his temples. Would the guy never stop?

"A crew digging beneath the Central Artery, the freeway that cuts through downtown, recently uncovered one of the lanterns. I have a photograph somewhere." He rummaged through his desk and came out with a Polaroid of an old lantern, unremarkable, save for its wide base. Dane and Bones looked it over while the professor went on. "The city's excavating the tunnel for the new submerged highway as part of what the newspapers are calling the 'Big Dig.' Workers have found a myriad of things underneath: timbers from sunken ships, Colonial-era plates and silverware, children's dolls. You name it, they found it."

"Jimmy Hoffa?" Bones asked.

Dane ignored Bones. "How do you think the lantern got there?"

"We can only speculate. Back in January, 1919, there was an incident in the North End section called the Boston Molasses Disaster. Some old-timers refer to it as the Boston Molassacre." Bones smiled at that. "A tank full of molasses exploded, due to a drastic change in air temperature, and sent a literal tidal wave of, forgive the pun, rapidly-moving molasses through the streets of the North End."

"Sweet!" Bones exclaimed.

"It must have been." Remillard opened a desk drawer and pulled out a manila folder full of yellowed newspaper clippings. He opened it and, right on the top, lay an article from the old *Boston Post*. It showed a street swamped with molasses. He passed it to Bones, who read the article with interest as Remillard continued. "Twenty-one people died, and one hundred-fifty were injured in the accident. Several buildings were swept off their foundations, and one of the elevated trains on Commercial Street went off the rails. The molasses traveled at about thirty-five miles per hour with two tons of pressure behind it. It decimated a good portion of that neighborhood.

"One of the buildings in the area was home to a descendant of Sexton Robert Newman, the man who, in April, 1775, hung the lanterns in the steeple of Old North Church, or Christ Church, and waited to see if the British would come by land or by sea. The church was ideal for the purpose, as it is highly visible, even sometimes serving as a lighthouse."

"They came by sea, right?" Bones asked.

"Correct. This served to alert not only Revere, but

also the militia in nearby Charlestown. If they let the lanterns burn too long, the British would see them, and all would be lost. Anyway, getting back to the molasses story, the lantern must have been in the man's house until the molasses swept it, and perhaps all of the man's possessions, away. Sometime during the excavation, a worker found it. Not knowing its value, but recognizing it as an antique, he took it home. Eventually, it found its way to the Old State House, where it's now on display."

"Where's the second lantern?" Dane asked.

"Missing. No one has seen it since shortly after the Midnight Ride."

"What does speculation say?"

Remillard smirked.

"History, not speculation, tells us that after the lanterns were extinguished that night, the redcoats caught the sexton carrying the second one down the stairs. They arrested him and seized the lantern, then brought it aboard *H.M.S. Somerset*, which lay at anchor nearby. *Somerset* took part in several important battles, but she was lost two and-a-half years later when she ran aground and foundered off the coast of Cape Cod."

"So the lantern is somewhere on the bottom of the North Atlantic." Bones chewed his lip, clearly mulling over the implications.

"It's possible, but the people of Truro and Provincetown divided up the spoils of the wreck."

"So it could also be that someone has the second lantern and doesn't even know it." Bones sounded discouraged at the thought.

"What's so important about finding this lantern?" Dane asked. "The historical significance?" His heart raced. Despite his skepticism, this mystery from Colonial times had him intrigued.

"Nick would have been the better person to answer that question." Remillard stroked his goatee, his eyes downcast. "He hinted that Revere was sitting on important, perhaps even dangerous knowledge, and said the lanterns were the keys, with emphasis on the *key*."

"Did either of you ever study the lantern that *has* been found?"

"Not yet. Nick applied for permission to study it, but hadn't gotten approval. He wasn't concerned—he said we needed both lanterns in order to solve the mystery. "

Dane considered this. Remillard seemed like a level-headed man, not at all prone to wacko theories. And, if Dane were honest with himself, he had to admit he was dying to get to the bottom of this mystery. Besides, he had given his word.

"Can you tell us anything else? I know it's not truly our mystery to solve, but I did give my word."

"Only that he had been acting oddly the past few days. He seemed to think he was in danger. "

Dane glanced at Bones and could tell they were thinking the same thing. Had Andrews' death truly been an accident?

"Otherwise," Remillard continued, "Nick was secretive about his project. I suspect he planned to tell me more last night, had he made it to our meeting. He has a daughter who only recently came back into his life. She might know more than I." He scribbled a name and phone number on a sheet of paper and handed it to Dane. "Please let me know if you find the lantern." He shook hands first with Dane, then with Bones. "I'd like to see Nick's work finished."

They thanked him for his help and left the office.

"I need to find the university library, and then I'm going to call Andrews' daughter. I know it's not how you wanted to spend our leave time, but are you up for a little detective work?"

"Looking for a two-hundred year old lantern and maybe running afoul of dangerous men?" Bones fixed him with a blank stare that, moments later, split into a broad grin. "I'm in!"

CHAPTER 5

"This chick we're meeting, do you think she's cute?" Bones winked at a pair of redheads who were walking along the street, headed in the opposite direction. One giggled and slowed a step, but her friend took her by the hand and hurried her along.

"I have no idea." Dane had followed up on the only lead Remillard could give them. Andrews' daughter initially greeted his call with suspicion but, when he explained the situation and mentioned Remillard's name, she warmed up enough to agree to a meeting.

"Did she sound skinny? I don't like skinny women. Well, they aren't my favorite."

Not for the first time, Dane wondered if Bones was doing all this just to get under Dane's skin.

The smell of fish hung in the hot air as they crossed beneath the Central Artery and downtown Boston unfurled before them. Crossing the uneven cobblestones that paved the area around Quincy Market, they stopped in front of Faneuil Hall.

Built in 1742, the three-story brick structure had served as both a meeting house and marketplace, and was one of America's most renowned historical landmarks. A grasshopper weather vane, a tourist favorite in its own right, perched atop the golden dome and white cupola. Dane and Bones found seats near the statue of Samuel Adams, cousin to John Adams and the original lieutenant-governor of Massachusetts, and settled into wait.

"I think this might be her." Bones indicated an attractive young woman. "Nice."

Dane had to agree. She moved with a grace that made her seem to walk on air, rather than paving stones. She wore a tight T-shirt and snug fitting jeans with the cuffs up around her calves. She wore her black hair tied up in a ponytail, and clutched a battered leather satchel as if her life depended on it.

She stopped a few paces away and pushed her sunglasses up to rest atop her head, revealing pale blue eyes. "Mister Maddock?"

Before Dane could reply, Bones stepped in, grabbed her hand, and held it gently. "That's Maddock, and I'm his best friend, Bones. It's a pleasure to make your acquaintance, Miss Andrews."

"You can call me Jillian."

"Can I carry your bag for you, Jillian?" Bones reached for the satchel, but Jillian pulled it tight against her chest.

"No." Her face tensed, then relaxed. "I'm sorry, it's just, I don't know you."

"How about we sit down for minute?" Dane patted the spot next to him. "We can get acquainted before we talk shop."

Jillian nodded and settled down next to Dane. Bones straddled a wrought iron armrest and looked down at them with interest.

"Like I said on the phone, we're very sorry for your loss," Dane began.

Jillian smiled, tears brimming in her eyes. "Thank you. I just finished up at the funeral home. No memorial service, no burial, according to his wishes. He wanted his ashes sprinkled in Boston Harbor on Independence Day." Tears welled in her eyes, so Dane changed the subject.

They filled the next few minutes with small talk, Dane and Bones telling Jillian about their service in the Navy, and she, in turn talking about her father and his interests. Finally, the conversation turned to the lantern.

"What can you tell us about this missing lantern?" Dane asked.

Jillian exhaled, her face downcast.

"I moved back home not long ago, and I quickly realized the lantern was Dad's passion, maybe you could call it his obsession." She paused. "And I suspect it was his downfall." She stared straight ahead, her eyes cloudy. "Some professors only want to write. Others just want to teach. Dad loved to search for history."

"What set him on this particular search?" Bones asked.

"He was always interested in the history of Boston: how she was formed, how the natives handled the influx of colonists..."

"I could tell you how natives feel about colonists,

but I don't want to sound like my grandfather." Bones' smile didn't reach his eyes.

One corner of Jillian's mouth twitched, but she came no closer to a smile than that. "He was fascinated with studying how Boston evolved from colony to town to city, especially leading up to the American Revolution. That was his favorite period in history."

"Mine too." Dane couldn't get enough of Colonial America and the Revolutionary War.

"Anyway, Dad spent most of his time focusing on the single most important aspect of our country's history: breaking away from King George and the throne of England. Of course, it all started April 18. 1775."

Dane and Bones listened as Jillian seemed to transform into a history professor. She spoke with the confidence of a well-educated woman. Dane figured her to be in her mid-thirties. She touched on many of the things Remillard had told them, but they didn't interrupt her. She seemed to find the experience cathartic, as if the retelling purged her painful memories.

"When the first lantern was rediscovered, he became a man possessed."

Dane scratched his chin and stared up at Samuel Adams. The mystery had taken hold of him, and he needed to solve it. He leaned back a little to get a better look at Jillian. Something told him that behind that pretty face laid a strong, determined woman. In spite of her grief and apparent fear, she clearly had not given up on her father's research. Otherwise, she wouldn't have met them today.

"I know our involvement in this is strange, but I gave your father my word that I'd find the lantern. I won't deny, I'd probably want to do it anyway. I love the Colonial period and I've never solved a mystery before. I guess I just want to make sure you understand that we're not trying to steal his glory or anything. I just want to see this thing through."

Jillian narrowed her eyes and seemed to look through Dane. "I don't know why, but I feel like I can trust you. Besides, Dad had been getting weird phone calls. I'd feel better if I wasn't alone in this."

"So, you intend to search for the lantern?" Bones asked.

"I want to finish what he started."

"Right now, the only possible lead we have is the *Somerset*. Is there anything else you can tell us? Anything to point us in the right direction?"

"Not much. He was paranoid about his project, so he kept his knowledge in his head. However, I have this." Jillian opened the leather satchel and withdrew an item wrapped in a hand towel. She unwrapped it, and held it out for them both to see. Sunlight gleamed off its long silver surface.

"What is it?" Bones leaned in for a better look.

"It's a butter knife." Dane frowned, wondering why she would show them this.

"It's not just any butter knife," Jillian corrected. She turned it, hesitated for half a heartbeat, and handed it to Dane. "Look at it closely."

The knife felt surprisingly heavy, but was

otherwise unremarkable. He turned it over in his hands, and then held it up for a closer look. A pair of initials, clear as day, rested right above the hilt. "Whoa!"

"Did you see your reflection?" Bones asked. "I hate to break it to you, Maddock, but you're not that handsome."

"Take a look for yourself." Dane held the knife out so Bones could see the initials.

"What does P.R. stand for? Was this made in Puerto Rico?"

This time, Jillian did manage a smile. "Paul Revere. According to my father, this is a piece of flatware that he made for Samuel Adams sometime before the Revolution."

"How did your father get his hands on it?" Dane asked.

"He stole it."

"Huh?" Dane and Bones chorused a little too loudly for Jillian's liking. She looked around, as if searching for eavesdroppers.

"Sorry," Dane said.

"It's all right. I'm just on edge. Anyway, Dad stole this knife from the Paul Revere House." She lowered her voice as she spoke. "I don't know the whole story. He just said it was special, and he would put it to a better use than just lying there on display."

"What was so special about the knife?" Dane asked.

"There was something odd my father saw in it, though I don't know what."

"So he picked it up."

"And ran with it. His research indicated that Revere made place settings for many important men of that time: John Hancock, John Adams, and James Swan. Pretty much all the Sons of Liberty."

"It's got a weird edge to it," Bones observed. "Instead of the fine serrations on one side, like you'd normally see, the grooves are on both sides, and they're kind of square." He handed the knife back to Jillian. "What's the connection between this knife and the lanterns?"

"That's just it. He never told me." Tears once again welled in her eyes. "And now he's gone."

CHAPTER 6

"So, we have to figure out the connection between a butter knife and a lantern." Dane shook his head as if he couldn't believe what he had just said.

"Paul Revere made them both?" Bones asked.

"It is entirely possible," Jillian replied, back into teaching mode. "Revere also worked with brass, and if the other lantern is any indication, the second one would be made of the same material."

"That's not much of a connection though, is it?" Bones waved at a pesky swarm of gnats that had taken a liking to him.

"Did anyone get a good look at the first lantern when they found it? Were there any markings like this on it?" Dane asked, pointing to the Revere brand on the knife.

Jillian shrugged. "That, I couldn't tell you."

"Do you have anything else that could help us?"

Jillian reached back into the satchel and pulled out two items: a folded map, as well as a hardcover book entitled *Historic Lighthouses of Cape Cod*. She handed both over to Dane.

He immediately opened the map. Bones looked

over his shoulder.

"What is it?" Bones asked.

"It's a map of the Freedom Trail," Jillian said. The Freedom Trail incorporated many of Boston's most important historical sites, and numbered among the city's most popular tourist destinations.

"There are some spots that have an X drawn through them," Bones noted. "What's that about?"

"I suppose those are places that my father has already searched for the lantern."

Dane tapped his chin and looked over the map, noting the numerical locations and matching them up with the key in the lower right-hand corner. Many of the spots, the late Professor Andrews had searched. He had already marked out the Park Street Church, King's Chapel, the Old Corner Book Store, the Old South Meeting House, and the Boston Massacre site. He looked toward Faneuil Hall. The professor hadn't searched it yet, he thought.

"He didn't get to Faneuil Hall, though."

"The Paul Revere House is on the Trail." Bones pointed out its location in North Square, one block south of Hanover Street.

"Right," Dane added. "And he's already been there to find the knife."

"But there's no X. Neither is there an X on the Old North Church, Copps, Constitution or the Bunker Hill Monument. There's a whole mess of unsearched places here."

"At least he eliminated a few." Jillian sounded affronted.

"No written records?" Dane asked.

Jillian shook her head. "He's been busy, though. Yesterday, he went to the Old State House."

"Where the first lantern is," Bones said.

"He came home, dropped off the map, and went out to meet someone. Remillard, I guess."

"You're sure it's okay with you that we take up the search on his behalf?" Dane asked.

"I'd be grateful." She gave him a tired smile. "Where do you think we should begin?"

"Remillard gave us a clue—the wreckage of Somerset. We thought we'd see if we can't find the wreckage."

Just then, a shiny, black sedan pulled up to the curb. The passenger door opened, and a man dressed in jeans, an Oxford cloth shirt, and wraparound sunglasses stepped out. He looked around for a moment, and then his eyes locked on Dane and the others.

"I've seen him before" Jillian whispered. "He came by the house asking for Dad just a few days ago."

"Do you have a car nearby?" Dane asked, not turning his head. He kept his eyes on the newcomer. Another door opened, and another, similarly-garbed man exited.

"Yeah." Her voice trembled as she spoke.

"Bones, give her the book and the map. Let's get out of here. Jillian, you lead the way."

Bones and Jillian moved a split second before Dane saw the newcomer reach behind his back.

"Gun!" Dane shouted and took off after his

friends.

"Hey, stop!" The newcomer's yells chased them around Faneuil Hall toward Quincy Market.

"Hurry, you two!"

"I better not twist an ankle and spend the rest of my leave laid up," Bones barked.

"You'll spend the rest of our leave in the freaking cemetery if you don't shut up and haul ass right this second, Bones."

The trio ran hard as a bullet buzzed past them and smacked into the hard granite of the old market building. Dane hadn't heard the gunshot. They must be using a silencer.

"Faster!"

Another bullet buzzed past them, ricocheting off the cobblestones near Dane's feet. As long as they kept moving, a shot with a handgun at this distance would be difficult even for a talented marksman. Still, neither bullet had missed by much.

They turned the corner as a third shot barely missed Bones' heel.

"This is it." Jillian pointed to a shiny, new BMW parked in the shadow of the Central Artery.

"Give me the keys," Dane demanded as Jillian opened the driver's side door.

"I don't think so," she countered. "I know the city better than you."

Dane snatched the keys from her, vowing to apologize later, if they got out of this mess.

"Get in."

Jillian shot him a dirty look and reluctantly

climbed into the back seat, as Bones had already wedged his lanky frame into the passenger side. Dane got in, closed the door, and quickly started the car. He slammed the accelerator to the floorboard and peeled away from the curb.

"If you scratch my father's car, you're toast."

"I think we've got bigger fish to fry right now."

They shot through a yellow light, narrowly avoiding a taxi cab turning left. Gunning the engine, they left the blaring horn behind them.

"Hopefully they won't have time to regroup and come back." Dane's hands were tight on the wheel and adrenaline coursed through him. "The first one had to have been in the middle of the mall by the time we pulled away, and the second one wasn't too far behind."

Jillian squealed in fright as Dane made a hard right, barely touching the brakes.

"Don't worry. I'll try not to scratch the paint while I'm busy saving our lives."

"What I'm worried about is walking away from the pile-up you're about to cause."

Dane's cheek twitched.

Bones lowered the passenger visor and angled it to look out the rear window. "I don't see them back there. Bummer. I was ready for a chase."

"Maybe next time."

"So, where are we going?" Bones asked.

"We'll take Jillian somewhere safe, and then you and I have an appointment to keep this evening."

CHAPTER 7

The last rays of the setting sun caromed off the tall buildings of downtown Boston as Dane and Bones made their way to the old Charlestown Navy Yard on the shore of the Charles River. They'd set Jillian up at a local motel while they saw to their task.

They crossed the Charlestown Bridge and turned onto Constitution Drive, pausing to pay their respects to Old Ironsides along the way. Its mast lights shone down on the white pine mainmast and black and white hull.

"So, what's your big plan?" Bones asked as they continued on.

"An old friend of my dad's lives here in town, and he owns a dive boat. He's going to hook us up with the gear we need and take us out. There it is right there."

"Whoa," Bones gasped. "Check that out. When you said dive boat, I pictured something smaller."

The live-aboard craft measured a good eighty feet from bow to stern with a twenty-five foot beam and second-deck bridge. Dane admired its sleek lines and thought he would love to own a boat just like this when he left the service.

"Dane Maddock, you swarmy son of a sea dog!" A rough voice called out.

Marco Cosenza, an old Navy pal of Dane's father, Hunter Maddock, was a dark complected, meaty slab of a man with close cropped hair. His appearance and manner reminded Dane of Vince Lombardi. He lumbered down the gangplank and caught Dane up in a rough embrace. Dane clapped man on the back and pushed away before his ribs caved in.

"How the hell are you, son?"

"I'm doing well, coach." Cosenza had been his Little League coach when the two families had been stationed in the same city in Florida decades ago. "I really appreciate you helping us out."

"Glad to do it." He turned to Bones. "I guess Dane isn't going to introduce us. I'm Marco Cosenza." They shook hands and Cosenza looked Bones up and down. "Anybody ever tell you you're the biggest Indian they've ever seen?"

"Nope. You're the first. I'm Bones. Good to meet you. I just hope you have a dive suit to fit me."

"I think we can find something." Cosenza turned back to Dane. "You told me where you want to dive, but not what you're looking for."

"How about we go aboard and I tell you all about it?" He followed Cosenza to the gangplank and stopped at the bottom. "Permission to come aboard *Sea Foam*, sir?"

"Granted." Cosenza chuckled and waved them aboard.

"I like your boat." Bones looked it over with an approving smile. "Ever think about renting it out for parties? I'll bet I could get a band and fifty Hooters girls on here easy."

Cosenza threw back his head and laughed. "My wife would love that!"

"That's why I'm never getting married. Too much Bones to go around. I can't deprive the lovely ladies of all this."

"I like your friend. Where did you find him?"

"He's not my..." Dane's voice trailed away under Bones' expectant look. "We're in SEAL training together."

"How's that going, anyway?" Cosenza asked.

"So far, so good. We made it through BUDS. We've still got a way to go, though."

"I always knew you'd make something of yourself. I know your dad is proud of you. How's he doing anyway? I haven't heard from him lately."

"He's off in Nova Scotia doing his pirate research. I don't know why he goes back to the same place every summer. You'd think he'd exhaust the possibilities and move on to someplace else."

An odd look passed across Cosenza's face and vanished as quickly as it had come. "I'm sure he knows what he's doing. Come on, let's get going before the night gets away from us."

Within half an hour, Cosenza had piloted *Sea Foam* out beyond the mouth of Boston Harbor. The temperature quickly dropped a good fifteen degrees and Dane breathed deeply of the cool ocean air. As the dive boat churned through the water at fourteen knots, Dane and Bones brought Cosenza up to speed. The university library had held plenty of information about the sinking of the *Somerset*, and enough information about currents and the ocean bed around Massachusetts for him to make a solid guess as to the ship's present location.

"I doubt there's much of *Somerset* left to find. A wooden vessel down in the waters of the North Atlantic more than two hundred years?"

"It's not probable," Dane admitted, "but it's possible. In any case, there might be detritus strewn about, items left over from the wreck. They've even found cargo of ships from ancient Greece, and that's a lot older than what we're looking for."

"That's the Mediterranean. But, if you kids want to swim around down there in the dark, I won't stop you. Better get suited up. We're almost there."

They donned their Lycra suits, Dane's a bit baggy around the middle, and Bones' too short at the wrists and ankle, and checked their air tanks. The steel AL80 cylinders were in suitable condition and filled to their seventy-seven cubic feet capacity. Dane doubted they'd be down long enough to need it all, but they each took a pony tank just in case.

Cosenza stood on the deck, arms folded across his chest, a light breeze ruffling what remained of his hair. The searchlight from a nearby lighthouse, high above the shoreline, sliced the darkness with a beam of white light, stretching toward the east.

"We're smack dab on the coordinates you gave me. Ready to do this?"

"See you soon, Coach."

Dane and Bones made their final checks, donned their cylinders, and moved to the deck rail. Dane gave Cosenza a quick, two-fingered salute, and flipped backward into the water.

He activated his dive light and plunged into the ocean's inky depths, shivering as the cool water enveloped him. A beam of white lanced through the water nearby as Bones activated his own light. Kicking steadily, they went deeper into the darkness.

Their lights found the silt of the ocean floor minutes later. He kept his breathing regular as the respirator filled his lungs with sweet air. The two men stayed close to one another, sweeping their lights back-and-forth. As they swam, Dane saw nothing but a featureless seabed.

It did not take long for him to determine their search was likely to be in vain. If any part of *Somerset* had withstood the corrosive power of the salt water, it had likely been carried away, either by human hands or the strong current.

Bones' dive light blinked three times, and Dane kicked toward him. He followed the beam down to the seabed. He couldn't help but swallow a little extra air as his heart skipped a beat. He recognized the large, curving wooden object immediately. *Somerset*'s keel!

They swam down for a closer look at the relic that hadn't seen the dawn in two hundred fifteen years. The meager light shone on the ship's wooden ribs, the timbers emerging from the silt like fingers reaching up from the grave. There was, however, no cargo to be seen. They probed the silt, but found nothing.

Dane's sense of wonder at seeing this ship out of a pivotal point in America's history battled with his disappointment. He supposed he hadn't truly expected to find the lantern down here, but his meticulous personality required him to at least eliminate the possibility. Plus, it had afforded him the chance to do the thing he loved most: dive on a wreck.

Bones tapped him on the shoulder and pointed up toward the surface. Dane nodded and they followed their bubbles upward. As they ascended, he spotted not one, but two hulls floating above them. He broke the surface and his vision exploded with white light.

Bones spat out his mouthpiece and squinted. "What the hell, dude?"

"United States Coast Guard," a deep voice boomed. "Come aboard, and keep your hands where I can see them."

Bones looked at Dane. "Babes and bar-hopping are looking pretty good right now, aren't they?"

CHAPTER 8

"I still can't believe they let us go." Bones waved a slice of extra crispy bacon for emphasis. When the Coast Guard had accosted them the previous night, Dane, Bones, and Cosenza had all given the Coast the same story—that they were merely searching for the wreckage of the *Somerset*. They'd been released after a stern warning about the dangers of night diving. Thankfully, Bones hadn't mentioned the fact that they were in training to be Navy SEALS. Maxie wouldn't have approved of his charges running afoul of their Coast Guard brothers in arms.

"It wasn't my finest moment," Dane muttered, taking a sip of coffee.

"Neither was your driving yesterday. It's a good thing we weren't in a boat. There was no freaking lighthouse around to keep us off the rocks or, in yesterday's situation, those pedestrians you almost hit."

"I didn't almost hit any..." Dane paused, staring straight ahead. "What did you just say?" The pieces were suddenly falling into place.

Bones blinked. "I said you almost ran over pedestrians," he began, but Dane waved him off.

"Jillian, do you have the lighthouse book with you?"

"Sure," she replied. "Why?"

Dane signaled for the check and dug a few bills out of his wallet.

"I'll tell you on the way. Let's get out of here."

As they headed toward the coast, he filled Bones and Jillian in on what he had in mind.

"You got me thinking. Bones, remember what Professor Remillard told us about the Old North Church and how, in 1775, it was sometimes used as a..."

"A lighthouse," Bones breathed.

"*Lighthouses of Cape Cod.* Professor Andrews had this book for a reason." The book lay in Jillian's lap and he tapped the cover for emphasis.

"So you're thinking that just maybe..."

"That maybe when Somerset ran aground, and the people divvied up the spoils of the wreck, somebody might have put that lantern to use."

"There was a lighthouse right above where we were diving." Bones sounded eager.

"In North Truro?" Jillian asked. "Let me look it up." She thumbed through the pages. "Here it is. Highland Light." She read further, her eyes widening with excitement. "It dates back to Colonial times!"

"Let's check it out." Dane stepped on the gas pedal and they zoomed toward the outer cape.

Dune grasses flanked the path to the Highland

Light, which ran through the middle of a small, nine hole golf course. Several people were out on the greens, ignoring the stiff wind that whipped in from the ocean.

They continued to walk until they came to the lighthouse itself. Behind it lay the waters of the North Atlantic, which shimmered blue as the whitecaps rolled toward the shoreline. Painted white from top to bottom with a pair of small, red-roofed structures attached to its side, Highland Light made them pause and soak in its grandeur. The glass enclosure at the top reflected the sun's blistering midday rays.

They learned that a tour group had just entered the lighthouse, so Dane paid their admission, and soon they were climbing the wrought iron steps that wound their way up to the observation deck.

Dane ran his hand along the lighthouse's brick-and-mortar interior wall. It didn't look or feel like a Colonial Era structure. It seemed much newer. A sinking feeling washed over and he ascended the staircase without much enthusiasm, Bones and Jillian following along behind.

The tour guide, a short, stocky man with blue eyes and light brown hair, was well into his presentation when they reached the top of the tower. They hung back, listening politely as the man pointed out local landmarks and shared bits of trivia.

Dane looked out across Truro. The view of the town from this lighthouse atop the bluffs was spectacular, and the view of the ocean equally so. The cool salt breeze bathed his face and he smiled. Nothing was better than the sea.

"Nice, isn't it?" Jillian whispered.

"I could get used to this," Bones said. "Growing up in the mountains was cool, but I've always wanted to live at the beach. Maybe some day." His dark eyes took on a faraway look as he gazed out at the dark line of the horizon.

Dane had to agree. It was an odd feeling to discover he had anything in common with the big Indian.

"I noticed you arrive toward the end of the presentation. Do you have any questions about the light?" Dane turned to see the tour guide standing behind them. He had a friendly smile and an easy manner.

"As a matter of fact, I do. This lighthouse seems awfully sturdy to be from Colonial times. How old is it?"

"You're quite right. There has been a lighthouse at this location since 1797, but this particular lighthouse was constructed in 1857."

Dane saw his companions' faces fall along with his heart. His hunch had been wrong.

"So this isn't the original lighthouse?" Bones asked.

"No. The first building was wooden. Obviously, it wasn't built to last. It was replaced in 1831 with a stone structure, and then this lighthouse was built a little over a quarter century later."

"Does this lighthouse sit on top of the old one?" Bones asked hopefully.

The guide shook his head. "The original was

somewhere close by, but no one knows exactly where. Besides, it wasn't like it had a basement or a foundation to be built upon." He paused. "This lighthouse will soon be moved. Originally, we had five hundred feet between the light and the cliff, but erosion is threatening the building." He pointed to the north. "Over there, we lost forty feet in 1990 alone."

"So the spot of the original lighthouse might have already washed away." Bones grimaced and looked down as if the structure on which they now stood had given offense.

Dane felt like he was going to be sick. He had led them on a wild goose chase. And he had been so certain.

"About the original lighthouse," Dane began, "what sort of lights did they use? Were they typical oil lanterns?"

"It's not out of the question that some smaller lighthouses might have hung a few lanterns in a pinch, but the spider lamp was the standard of the day." He saw Dane's questioning expression and went on. "The spider lamp consisted of what amounted to a bowl of oil with several wicks, hence the nickname spider. Highland Light was a bit higher tech than most of its contemporaries. In an attempt to distinguish it from the Boston lighthouse, it was given a revolving reflector."

"So there's no way Highland Light used an old-school lantern?" Bones asked.

The guide shrugged. "As I said, maybe in a pinch. Perhaps if the keeper accidentally let the fire burn out and needed to hang a light while he went to get more oil, but it's not likely."

"I don't suppose there are any remnants or artifacts from the original lighthouse anywhere, are there?" Jillian asked.

"You might try the museum. They have a lot of Colonial Era items in the collection, some that belonged to previous keepers."

They thanked him for his help and descended the stairs in a funk.

"Do we try the museum?" Bones asked. His voice held no disappointment or accusation. "Might be worth a look."

"Might as well as long as we're here." Dane tried to keep his tone upbeat, but he failed. "I just hope I haven't wasted our time."

The Highland House Museum, operated by the Truro Historical Society, sat located a stone's throw from the lighthouse. A woman with iron gray hair and a stern manner greeted them politely, if without warmth, as they entered. Her name tag read "Anne Revere."

"Any relation to Paul?" Bones asked.

"As a matter of fact, I am a direct descendent." She smiled for the first time. "And proud of it. Didn't even take my first husband's name when we married. Drove him crazy. Of course, it also upset him that I insisted on referring to him as my *first* husband from the day of our wedding."

"That's cold." The twinkle in Bones' eyes

contradicted his words.

"I just had a feeling. Now, what brings you to the Museum?"

"We were wondering if you have any items in your collection associated with the original lighthouse," Jillian said. "I'm doing some research."

Revere furrowed her brow for the briefest of instants, but then her features smoothed. The reaction had been so brief, Dane wondered if the others had even noticed.

"There are a few items in the collection that are associated with the keepers of the early nineteenth century, but they are scattered about, and not all are labeled as such. Ours is not so much a lighthouse museum as a general one. Our collection can be broken down into several categories: Farming and Industry, Fishing and Whaling, Shipwrecks, Tourism, Artists, and Native American."

Dane noticed Bones' reaction when she mentioned shipwrecks. For a moment, he feared Bones wouldn't hold his tongue, but his worries were unnecessary. Bones didn't spill the beans.

"Thanks. We'll look around."

"Let me know if I can answer any questions." Revere gave them a perfunctory smile and retreated through a door behind the counter into a small office. The nameplate on the door named her Museum Director.

"Are you thinking what I'm thinking?" Bones asked softly.

Dane nodded. "*Somerset.*"

They were disappointed. There were no artifacts from *Somerset,* only a small display that included a model of the ship, a few paintings, a placard giving a brief summary of the wreck, and an old newspaper clipping about the opening of this particular display.

"Kind of hard up for news, aren't they?" Jillian sounded bitter.

"We might as well check the rest of the Museum." Dane didn't know why they were wasting their time. He despised failure, and the thought of it turned his stomach.

The others agreed to continue the search but, thirty minutes later, they were ready to give up. There were a few Colonial era lanterns, but none bearing Revere's mark."

"I was so sure too." Dane stood, arms folded across his chest, staring at the *Somerset* display.

"Don't worry about it, dude." Bones gave his shoulder a friendly squeeze. "We all make mistakes sometimes, even the mighty Dane Maddock."

Dane smiled, but not at the jibe. Something had caught his eye.

"You're right. I do make mistakes, but today is not the day." Heart pounding he moved back to the display and tapped the newspaper clipping. "Look at this photograph carefully. What do you see?"

Jillian gasped. "There was a lantern! And it's a dead ringer for the first Revere lantern."

"But where is it now?" Bones asked. "Stolen? Donated to another museum? It could be anywhere."

"I've got a feeling it's not too far away." Dane

enjoyed their twin confused expressions.

"Don't hold out on us," Jillian snapped.

"Remember, the lantern was made by Paul Revere. Who do we know who is descended from Revere and proud of it?"

Bones whistled.

"You don't think..." Jillian whispered.

"I think Maddock's right. I doubt she could've resisted making it part of her personal collection. Heck, I might have done the same thing. If I were in her shoes. She probably sees it as a family heirloom."

"But steal from the museum? She could be arrested."

"What if she didn't exactly steal it?" Dane asked.

Bones smiled broadly, putting his straight, white teeth on display. "I like your thinking, Maddock. Let's find out." He immediately took charge. "We'll spread out like we're all checking out different parts of the museum. Jillian, tell Revere you've got some questions about one of the displays. Make it the farthest from her office. You only need to keep her distracted for a couple of minutes, if that."

"Are you sure about this?" Dane asked.

"Relax. I've been walking the straight and narrow for a long time. It's about time I returned my roots, or at least paid them a visit." He gave them a roguish smile and wandered away.

Dane and Jillian exchanged exasperated looks before splitting up. He selected a room near the front office where he could keep an eye on things. He watched as Jillian lured Revere out of her office and back among the displays. Moments later, Bones, his leather jacket draped over his arm, slipped into the office. Dane kept a silent count in his head. The wait felt like an eternity, and he was surprised that he had only reached a count of thirty when Bones reemerged from the office, gave Dane a thumbs up, and slipped out the front door.

Dane couldn't believe their luck. Heart racing with anticipation and a measure of relief, he found Jillian and Revere, apologized for interrupting them, and told them it was time to head back to New York. To her credit, Jillian understood the ruse immediately. No harm in a little misdirection should Revere notice the lantern missing. They returned to the car as quickly as they could without drawing suspicion. Bones waited in the passenger seat, his jacket draped over something lying on the floor board.

"Took you long enough. Let's get the hell out of here."

Jillian's car had only a rear license plate, so Dane made a point of backing all the way out of the parking lot before turning around and gunning the engine. He doubted Revere had bothered to watch them leave, but this was his first grand theft, and he didn't want to leave anything to chance.

When they were well out of sight of the Museum, Bones reached underneath his jacket and drew out a lantern. "Maddock was right. It was sitting on top of the bookshelf by her desk. Check it out!" He flipped the lantern over, revealing a rectangular stamp with the name *Revere*.

"That doesn't look like the mark on the butter knife," Dane observed, glancing at the lamp before returning his eyes to the road.

"Revere used more than one mark." Jillian took the lantern from Bones. "This is one he used for larger items."

"I can't believe we found it," Dane said. "Next question: what happens when she notices it's missing? Won't the cops be on our tail in a matter of minutes?"

"Not unless she takes it down for a close inspection. I snagged one of the display lanterns and switched them out. She's so short, and the bookcase is so tall, that I doubt she'll notice the difference at a glance. I'm sure she'll figure it out sooner or later. Hopefully, it'll be some time down the road when we are all forgotten."

"Nice one." Dane frowned. Here he was, praising a man for the skill with which he engaged in criminal activity. Heck, paying Bones any sort of compliment felt strange.

"Thanks, bro." Bones took the lantern back from Jillian and turned it over in his big hands. "The base of this thing is weird. It's got a cross running through it." He held it up for them both to see.

"Some of Revere's artistry, I imagine," Jillian said.

"You know, after we've solved the mystery, no reason we can't return them anonymously."

"Them?" Dane spared Bones a quizzical glance.

"We need the other lantern. As long as I'm in a thieving mood, I guess we should figure out how to get our hands on it."

"Actually, I've been thinking about that." Jillian spoke slowly, as if choosing her words with care. "An ex-boyfriend of mine used to work for the transit system. We had a special place to meet while he was on break."

"What say you show it to me later?" Bones leered at her.

"I don't know." She flashed a coy smile. "I still haven't decided which of you is cuter."

Dane felt the back of his neck grow hot and he hoped they didn't see his face redden. It wasn't that he felt shy around women. He was just... reserved. He noticed Bones gazing at him, and fixed his eyes firmly on the road. It wouldn't do for the two of them to get into it over Jillian just when they were starting to get along.

"I can answer that for you." Bones said. "Maddock is cuter; I'm hotter. Think of us as a buffet."

"All you can eat." Dane didn't know where that comment had come from, but Bones chortled.

"Maddock! You made a joke! A good one, too."

"Who says I was joking?" Dane managed to keep a straight face, which only made Bones laugh all the harder.

Jillian's exasperated sigh cut through the frivolity. "If you two clowns will get serious. I'll tell you my idea."

Dane listened as she outlined her plan. He couldn't believe that, for the second time that day, he was planning a burglary. He'd hoped to rub off on Bones in a positive way, but the tables had been turned.

Surprisingly, he was enjoying himself. When Jillian finished, he thought it over for a minute.

"All right. Let's give it a shot."

CHAPTER 9

Their footsteps echoed through the Blue Line tunnel beneath Bowdoin Station. Dane looked down at the narrow walkway, scarcely wide enough for them to pass, and wondered why he'd agreed to this crazy idea. Should a car come along at an inopportune time, he doubted any of them could flatten against the wall tightly enough to avoid being roadkill.

The latest car had left the station only seconds before, and Jillian had assured them it was only a short way to the turnoff. Their mini Maglites sliced through the darkness, illuminating the damp tunnel and gleaming rail line.

They came to a battered door marked *Danger. Do Not Enter.*

"It's perfectly safe," Jillian whispered. "This leads to a mechanical room that's no longer in use. My ex put this sign here to discourage unwanted visitors." She grimaced. "Come to think of it, I wouldn't be surprised if the loser is living under here. Hope he hasn't changed the locks." She fished a key out of her pocket, unlocked the door, and tugged on it, but it did not budge.

"Let me get that." Bones gently removed her hands from the doorknob, took hold of it himself, and yanked it open. The door drew back with a loud, scraping sound that reverberated through the empty tunnel.

She led them down the dank passageway and into a room thirty feet square. Exposed wires dangled from the ceiling, and various conduits and electrical boxes lined the far wall.

"Doesn't look like anyone's found your love nest," Dane said.

"I don't think he's been back." Jillian walked to the corner and nudged a bundle with her toe. "The air mattress is right where I left it."

"Have I told you you're my kind of girl?" Bones tried to slip his arm around her shoulders but she moved away.

"I *was* your kind of girl. That is, if you like them young and stupid."

"Pretty much."

Jillian rolled her eyes.

"Where do we go from here?" Dane looked around for another door.

"Straight up." She pointed toward the ceiling. "Give me a boost?" She moved to the far wall and took hold of a conduit. Dane cupped his hands and, when she stepped in, hauled her up until she stood atop an electrical box. "Follow me, boys."

Dane was an experienced climber and had no trouble following as she scrambled up into the ceiling. He glanced back to make sure Bones was keeping pace.

"Hurry it up, Grandpa. I'm going to fall asleep waiting for you."

"I believe I outclimbed you every time in training." Dane had no idea if that was true, but he wasn't about to admit it.

"Today's opposite day? Next time we're on leave, I'm taking you back to North Carolina. We'll head up into the mountains and see who's the better climber."

"Sounds good." Dane realized he halfway meant it. Rock climbing in the Appalachians sounded like fun, even if it did involve Bones.

"I'll introduce you to my sister. All my friends think she's cute, but they're scared to make a move."

"Afraid you'll kick their asses?"

"No. Afraid she will."

"Maybe I don't want to meet your sister after all." Dane winced at the sudden mental image of Bones in a dress.

"If you two Marys are done gabbing, we're almost there. Stay right behind me." Jillian scrambled ahead.

They crawled forward for a good twenty yards, Bones muttering all the while about Dane getting the "better view." Finally, they came to a stop in front of a metal vent. They fell silent, listening for voices or footsteps, but the only sound he heard was the whir of a refrigerator.

"It's the employee break room in the Old State House," Jillian explained. "My boyfriend and I used to climb up here and steal food." She pushed the vent free and slid out into the room. Dane followed, scarcely managing to squeeze his shoulders through.

"I don't think you're going to make it," he told Bones.

"Watch me. I've been spelunking all my life and I've squeezed through cracks smaller than this." He paused, staring at Dane.

"What?"

"Squeezed through cracks? Dude, I serve you up a fat pitch like that and you don't knock it out of the park?" Shaking his head, he wormed his way through the gap and stood. "Still got work to do on you, Kemosabe."

Dane ignored him. He opened the break room door an inch and peered out into the dark, silent hallway.

"Lights out." He turned off his Maglite and Bones followed suit.

"Why?" Jillian whispered.

"I've got excellent night vision, and there's plenty of light from the street to see by." He moved out into the hallway and crept silently through the darkness. Jillian had confirmed that the doors were alarmed, but the building had no interior alarm system. At least, there had not been one when she'd explored the building in years past.

They halted at the doorway that opened into the display room and peered inside. The lone security camera was mounted above them, aimed toward the main entrance.

Bones slipped his jacket off and tossed it up onto the camera. It took two tries, but it finally hung there. "No video evidence."

"Jillian, watch the front door," Dane whispered. As she hurried across the room, they moved to the lantern.

It sat in a plexiglass box atop a pedestal. He gazed at it in the dim light that filtered through the windows. There were still streaks of dark brown encrusted within its seams. Whoever had tried restoring it to 1775 condition had failed to remove all of the molasses. There was little in the way of glass left within it, and Dane couldn't help but wonder how much abuse the lantern had suffered, stuck underground for so many years.

"So there it is," he whispered. "The lantern that helped kick off our revolution. Well, one of the lanterns, at any rate. The one that wasn't captured by the British that night."

"Yep. There it is, all right."

"You ever been this close to history before, Bones?"

"Yeah, I have," Bones replied.

Dane didn't turn his head, but he heard the sobering tone, and he knew it took something significant to make Bones adopt such a serious note.

"I'm sure I'm going to regret this, but what was it?"

"I held Booth's Derringer."

Dane snapped his head around. "Wow. How'd you manage that?"

Bones never took his eyes off the lantern. "They were cleaning the displays when some of my friends and I were walking through the theater. One of the workers left the case open, so I walked over and grabbed it."

"How long did you hold it?"

"A few seconds. Wish I could have fired it. That would have rocked."

"There's someone outside!" Jillian's soft voice carried through the empty hall.

"Time to get to work." Bones took out a set of tiny metal tools on a ring which he'd picked up at an auto parts store. "Feeler gauge," he explained.

"If you say so."

Selecting one of the tools, Bones slid it into the lock and worked it. Moments later, the lock turned. "Wafer locks. Not even a challenge."

"How did you do that?"

"As I have said many times, it's a product of a misspent youth. Nowadays, I only use my powers for good. Or for fun."

"Maybe hanging out with a reformed criminal isn't the worst thing in the world." Careful not to leave fingerprints, Dane opened the case, took out the lantern, and slipped it into a drawstring backpack, then replaced the lantern with a folded card reading,

"THIS ITEM TEMPORARILY OFF DISPLAY"

It wouldn't fool anyone for long, but it might delay the moment someone discovered the theft. Sweat pouring down the back of his neck, he called to Jillian. When she joined them, Bones retrieved his jacket, and Dane led the way back to their escape route.

"You okay, Maddock?" Bones frowned at him, genuinely concerned.

"It's stupid, but this is my first theft. I mean, I was technically an accomplice on the last one, but this time, I'm the one who actually took the lantern and carried it away."

Jillian and Bones exchanged stunned glances.

"Not even a candy bar when you were a kid?" Jillian asked.

"Or a car when you were in junior high?" Bones took a step away from the others and held up his hands. "Don't hate. It was a special occasion."

Dane sighed. "Just when I was starting to think you were all right."

Bones gave him a high five. "I'll straighten you out yet, Maddock. How about we go back to Jillian's and see what's up with these lanterns?"

CHAPTER 10

While he believed they had gotten away clean, Dane kept checking his rear-view mirror for blue lights. He didn't completely relax until they pulled up in front of a tall brownstone.

"Home, sweet home." Jillian's voice held a note of sadness. "My grandfather bought it in the 1940's, and Daddy inherited it some thirty years ago." Her voice cracked. "I may end up selling it and find a small place for me somewhere else. Too many bad memories here."

Dane searched for words of comfort, but he couldn't imagine the pain of losing a parent. Before he could think of something to say, his sharp eyes spotted something amiss.

"Did you see that?" He pointed at an upstairs window. "A flicker of light, like someone's in there with a flashlight."

"I don't see anything." Jillian's voice was tight.

"Bones and I will go in first. Stay close to us."

They walked in, but Dane didn't let Jillian get too far inside, holding his hand out to keep her back. He suddenly wished he had his Walther P99. Oh well, nothing to be done about it now. He shut the door, careful not to let the click of the lock echo through the house.

Dane headed upstairs, taking each step with care. The third step from the top squeaked, causing him to pause and flinch. He filled his lungs with air and continued to the landing, wishing he had a weapon.

His heart hammering away, he eased into the room where he'd seen the light. The dull light from the streetlamp out front provided ample light, enough to see this was a study or office of some sort. Bookcases lined the walls, and a small desk sat in the bay window facing the street. The drawers were open and their contents strewn across the floor. Whoever had been there had gone. Dane and Bones made a quick search of the rest of the upstairs rooms with no success. When Dane turned to head downstairs, he noticed Jillian's absence.

"Where'd she go?" he whispered.

"I don't know. She was waiting in the hall a few seconds ago."

A loud crash followed by an agonized scream broke the silence.

They pounded down the stairs, the screams echoing through the darkness. They reached the first floor and darted into the living area. Dane flipped on the light to reveal Jillian and a skinny man tangled on the floor. She had him in an ankle lock, pouring all her strength into flattening out the man's foot. From the looks of things, and the way the man kept screaming and pounding his fists on the floor, she had already done some serious damage.

"Jillian!" Dane yelled. "Let go of him."

"No!"

"He's not going anywhere. We won't let him." Dane's thoughts raced. Who was this guy and what did he want? He didn't look like the men who had chased them the previous day.

"You got me, you got me," the man wailed.

Bones grabbed Jillian and wrenched the man free from her grasp, pulling her away as Dane moved in quickly and stood over the fallen man.

"You try to run, and I'll make what she did to you feel like a massage. You get me?" The man nodded and Dane grabbed his shoulder. "Get up."

The intruder rose gingerly. After patting him down and finding nothing in the form of a weapon, Dane shoved him into a nearby chair. The man, favoring his injured ankle, nearly fell. He slumped down, glaring at Dane.

He was a weedy fellow with a patchy black beard and receding hair of the same color. His lip curled in a sneer, and he breathed hard through his nose. Perhaps he thought it a tough look, but his Vanilla Ice t-shirt ruined the effect.

Dane looked to Bones and saw Jillian break away from an embrace and hurry into the adjoining kitchen. He felt a brief pang of something, maybe jealousy, but suppressed it.

"She okay?" he asked.

"Yep."

Dane firmed his jaw and turned back to the intruder. "Who are you and what are you doing here?"

The man remained defiantly silent.

Bones brushed past Dane, smiled at the man, then struck him hard across the ear with his open hand. Their captive raised a hand to the side of his head and Bones kicked him in the stomach. The fellow doubled over and retched.

"Jillian," Bones called, "you got salad tongs and a corkscrew in there?"

"Yeah, why?" Her voice was weak. Clearly, the break-in had shaken her.

"This dude needs a little eye surgery."

"What are you gonna do to me?" Panic washed over the intruder's face.

"Just something my ancestors have been doing to white men for centuries. I have to tell you it hurts. A lot."

He blanched and a frightened moan escaped his lips.

Jillian re-entered the room, not looking at the intruder, and handed over the utensils.

"Grab me a knife, too, in case I want to scalp him." Bones rubbed his hands together in anticipation while the man continued to moan. "Oh, shut up. Stop being a little wuss."

"I guess we should call the police," Dane said.

"Not yet. First, I want to extract some information."

"Yeah, just question him and let him go," Jillian called from the kitchen. "No need to involve the cops."

Dane wanted to argue, but he thought he understood her reasoning. If the fellow knew about the lanterns, talking to the police could impede their search and potentially link them to the thefts. "I'm going to ask again. What's your name?"

The fellow's lips moved, but he uttered no sound. Running out of patience, Dane grabbed him by the front of the shirt, hauled him to his feet, and relieved him of the contents of his pockets: a flashlight, wallet, and Swiss army knife. He took out the license and read the name aloud.

"Roger Drinkel."

"All right, Roger," Bones shoved him back into the chair, "I've got questions for you, but first I've got to tell you why you're stupid. You know why I'm going to do that?"

Drinkel shook his head.

"Because I hate stupid people. Almost as much as I hate rednecks. First off," he held up a finger, "never use a flashlight. Pull the curtains and turn the light on. People come home, they see a light on inside the house, they figure they just forgot to turn it off. They see a flashlight beam flickering around, they know something's up."

Drinkel's facet turned a deep shade of red.

"Second, never carry your ID with you. Do I need to explain why?"

Drinkel held his silence, staring up at Bones through eyes that burned with resentment.

"Cool, now that we've gotten that out of the way, here's what's going to happen. You're going to tell me who you're with and why you're here. You leave anything out, or give me reason to believe you're lying, I'm going to hurt you until I'm bored, then kill you and dump your body in the Charles River. You ready to talk?

Drinkel looked from Bones to Dane, gulped, took a deep breath, and let it out in a rush. His resolve deflated like a balloon.

"All right, but you didn't hear this from me."

CHAPTER 11

"I'm a Son of the Republic." Despite his present circumstances, Drinkel sat up straighter and his eyes shone when he made the proclamation. "And we are going to make things right with America."

Dane and Bones exchanged scornful glances.

"You people don't get it." Drinkel hadn't missed their expressions. "The depravity is coming to an end. It has been foretold."

"By whom?" Dane asked.

"You mean who," Bones said.

"What?"

"Isn't it 'who' when it's an object, or is it the other way around?"

"Who cares?" Dane could tell by Drinkel's smirk that they were losing their intimidation factor. Bones must have noticed too, because he casually backhanded the man across the face.

"True, we've got more important things to focus on." Bones turned to Drinkel. "Tell us about this prophecy. Who made it and when? Some doomsday freak back in 1984?"

"Would you call the father of our country a

freak?"

Dane guffawed. "The so-called Prophecy of George Washington? That's a legend."

"What am I missing here?" Bones frowned at Dane.

"There's a legend that, at Valley Forge, George Washington was visited by an angel who prophesied three great trials for America. Ah!" Something had just clicked. "The angel addressed him as 'Son of the Republic.' I take it that's where your little club got its name?"

"Our order," Drinkel, "traces its heritage from the Sons of Liberty. We are America."

"Yeah, whatever." Bones dismissed him with a wave, but Drinkel flinched, apparently expecting to be hit again. "So, what were these trials?"

"It's all crap. It was written around the time of the Civil War by an author who wrote similar things for a lot of figures from history. Supposedly, the first trial was the American Revolution, the second the Civil War, and the third, the most grave, had the nations of the world uniting beneath a black cloud. America teeters on the brink, but we pull together and win in the end."

Now it was Drinkel's turn to laugh. "That's the prophecy you think you know. The true one, handed down from the days of our Founding Fathers, tells a different story."

"And what would that be?" Dane was sure the guy was a nutter, but there had to be a connection between his presence here and search for the lanterns.

"The threat comes from within. The government is corrupt, prostituting itself to the lowest of the low. It must be brought down and rebuilt according to the vision of the Fathers. We will open the Gate of Freedom and all true patriots will come charging through to reclaim our nation."

"If you already know what the prophecy says, why do you need to find it?"

Drinkel hesitated but hurried on when Bones started playing with the corkscrew. "Some of our members hold back. They need proof that the time to strike is now. Once the prophecy is revealed, others will flock to our cause. America's eyes will be opened."

"Open to what a freak you are."

"And you think Professor Andrews had this prophecy?" Dane asked.

"I thought he might have the key."

Dane went cold. If Drinkel knew about the lanterns, they had a big problem. "What key would that be?"

"*She* doesn't know?" Drinkel glanced at the kitchen door.

"She's just seeing to her father's estate. That's all."

Drinkel made a face. "The key is the diary of Samuel Adams."

"The beer guy?" Bones asked. "What are you looking for? Recipes?"

Drinkel smirked. "Her father knew. I'm surprised he didn't trust her enough to tell her." He saw the angry look on Dane's face and continued. "The Founding Fathers all knew the prophecy, and Adams recorded it in his journal. There are subtle mentions of it in his other writings."

"And you thought the professor found it?" Dane asked.

"If not the diary, then perhaps clues to its location. He's an expert and he's been walking the red line, after all."

The phrase sounded familiar, but Dane couldn't recall where he'd heard it.

"I've got a question," Bones said. "Why did they send an idiot like you to find it?"

"My comrades moved too slowly for my liking. I'm not afraid to take action."

"Do you have any clues as to where the diary might be?"

At this, Drinkel's face went blank and he stared resolutely at the opposite wall.

"He asked you a question." Bones took a threatening step toward the man, but Drinkel's face remained impassive. Bones struck him again on the side of the head, but he scarcely acknowledged the blow. "Time for me to use this?" Bones brandished the corkscrew.

"No. I think it's time to call the cops." Dane looked around for the telephone.

Jillian poked her head through the kitchen door. "Are you sure we shouldn't let him go?"

Bones frowned, clearly not liking the idea.

Dane considered it. The police, once they heard Drinkel's far-fetched story, would likely consider him just another whacked-out conspiracy theorist. He hadn't mentioned the lanterns and, even if he knew about them, Dane doubted he would say anything to the authorities. Most likely, he'd be charged with burglary, and released after posting a modest bail. It would at least buy some time for them to continue their search. He turned to Jillian.

"Make the call."

After the police hauled Drinkel away, Dane, Bones and Jillian sat around the kitchen table sipping coffee.

"What do you think?" Bones asked.

"I think he's added a wrinkle to the mystery." Dane mulled the problem over. "I definitely think there's a connection between the journal and the lanterns."

"What makes you say that?" Bones looked at him sharply.

"First of all, he mentioned opening the gates of freedom. The professor said the same thing to me."

"I can remember Daddy saying it. Also, I swear I've seen it written somewhere."

"Second, did you notice his tattoo?" Bones and Jillian shook their heads. Dane took hold of one of the lanterns, both of which were sitting on the table, and turned it over so they could get a good look at the oddly-shaped base. "The crossed circle that Bones pointed out to us. Drinkel had this shape tattooed on his chest. I noticed when I grabbed him by the shirt."

"What does it symbolize?" Bones asked.

"I don't know. It's a Celtic symbol, but I guess it

means something different to him."

"Maybe it's a symbol of the Sons of the Republic," Jillian offered.

"That's what I'm thinking."

"What did he mean by Andrews has been walking the red line?" Bones looks back and forth between the two of them. "If he meant the Johnny Cash song, he got the lyrics all wrong."

"He means the Freedom Trail," Jillian said. "It's a red brick trail, so people call it the red line." Her eyes widened. "You know what? I think that's where I saw the phrase 'gates of freedom.' Let me check."

She dug into the satchel and retrieved Andrews' map of the Freedom Trail. Sure enough, someone, probably Andrews, had jotted *The Gates of Freedom?* in small, spidery script at the bottom.

"It doesn't seem to denote any particular spot," Dane noted, "but he apparently thought it was somewhere on here. He didn't leave any other notes about it?"

"Like I said, he preferred not to write things down."

"Okay. How about we put that on the back-burner for a minute and work on the clues we do have?" Bones indicated the lanterns.

"Definitely." Dane looked at Jillian. "Any ideas?"

"Well," she bit her lip, "I examined the first one pretty thoroughly on the way home and I didn't see anything promising on the outside, nor in the obvious places, like the oil reservoir or the area around the wick. If either lantern hides a clue, it's hidden somewhere on the inside."

Dane hesitated, uncomfortable with the idea of taking apart such an important artifact. Then again, he didn't have much choice."

"Either you do it or I will." The eagerness was evident in Bones' face. He loved demolition or destruction of any kind.

"Fine." Dane held the lantern up to the light and looked it over with tired eyes. Finally, he took a deep breath, grabbed hold of the base, and twisted.

Nothing.

"Pitiful." Bones shook his head. "Remind me never to ask you to make me a peanut butter sandwich. You'd never get the jar open."

Dane grimaced. "What if it's not meant to open, and I break it?"

"That would actually be a good thing."

"Bones, be serious."

"I am. If that thing's not meant to open, that means the clue, if there is one, is still inside."

Bones had a point. Dane turned the lantern over again, gazing at Paul Revere's mark, and something caught his eye. "I'm an idiot. There's a thin slot right next to the printer's mark."

"I noticed that earlier," Jillian said. "You think it's significant?"

Dane's skin tingled and his heart raced, and his mind now fired on all cylinders. He'd just made a connection.

"Where's the butter knife?"

Jillian gaped and Bones smacked himself on the

forehead. She took the knife out of the satchel and passed it over with trembling hands.

Dane slid the knife into the slot until it stopped, then gave it a clockwise turn. Something clicked, and the knife slid free.

"Okay, here goes." This time, he took a firm grip and twisted with all his might. It held for a moment, and then something broke loose and the base turned. Smiling he continued twisting and the bottom of the lamp unscrewed. He could scarcely breathe while he removed it and looked inside.

"What do you see?" Jillian's soft voice held a note of breathy eagerness.

"Nothing." The inside of the base was empty. "When it came loose, I was so sure." He gazed down into it and something caught his eye. "Wait a minute! Jillian, do you have a magnifying glass?"

"Daddy had one he used to read books with fine print." She hurried out of the room and returned with it a few moments later.

Dane peered through the glass. He saw a tiny circle of engraving, its circumference not much larger than a half-dollar.

"Anything?" Bones sounded wary. He likely didn't want to be disappointed again.

"I see the circle-and-cross and then..." Dane turned the base in his hand. "I see the alphabet and the numbers 0-9."

"Crap!" Bones banged his fist on the table, nearly upending their coffee cups. "Sorry. I got my hopes up." Then he saw the expression on Dane's face. "I must be missing something, because you look pleased with yourself."

"What are you thinking, Maddock?" Jillian asked with a hint of trepidation.

"During the Revolution and in the pre-Revolutionary era, heck, throughout history, people have passed along secret messages using..."

"Ciphers!" Jillian exclaimed.

"And I'll bet you a Dos Equis the other half of the key is inside the second lantern."

"Sweet!" Bones was already working the knife into the bottom of the other lantern, which was putting up solid resistance after its long immersion in molasses and who knew what else? Finally, he succeeded in opening it, and handed the base to Dane.

"There it is. A ring of symbols. We've got it!"

"Could that be the connection?" Jillian rose to her feet and began pacing. "We need the cipher to decode a message in Adams' journal?"

"Makes sense to me." Dane sprang to his feet. "And if you've got a phone book, I've just thought of someone who might be able to help us."

CHAPTER 12

Jimmy Letson lived in a third-story apartment on Boston's South End in sight of the Hancock Building. He had befriended Dane early in Dane's first year in the Navy. Shortly thereafter, Jimmy had entered, and rung out of, SEAL training. At the end of his tour of duty, he had returned to his native Boston and become a journalist, but it wasn't his journalistic skills Dane needed right now.

Jimmy answered the door on the first knock. A tall, wiry man with unkempt curly brown hair and a wispy mustache, he gazed at them through bleary eyes.

"Seriously, Maddock? It's the middle of the night, and you expect me to drop everything and help you with a research project?"

"It's not a research project, it's... I don't know what to call it, but it's important. Besides, I come bearing gifts." He held out a bottle of Scotch he'd found in Andrews' liquor cabinet.

Jimmy accepted the bottle and peered at it over his John Lennon-style glasses. He didn't actually need them; he just liked the way they looked. "White Label. Surprisingly good taste for a beer guy. All right, come on in." He didn't bother holding the door for them, but turned and strode back into the apartment.

Jimmy had furnished his living room in early 1970s thrift store: lots of browns, oranges, and dark wood. A framed *Star Wars* movie poster, the sole concession to artwork, hung above an overstuffed bookshelf.

Jimmy motioned for them to sit down, then headed into the kitchen and returned with four glasses. While Jimmy poured them all drinks, Dane introduced his companions.

Bones accepted the glass of Scotch, frowned at it, then looked up at Jimmy. "Did anyone ever tell you that you look like Weird Al?"

"Did anyone ever tell *you* that you look like a cigar store Indian?"

"Cheers!" Bones clinked glasses with Jimmy, settled back into his chair, and took a drink. His face contorted and he shuddered. "Holy crap! How do white people drink this stuff?"

"You get used to it." Dane turned to Jimmy. "You said you found something for us?"

"I love how you get right down to business. It's the first time you seen your old friend in years, and you don't even bother to ask what I've been up to."

"I know what you been up to: writing for the *Globe*, playing Dungeons & Dragons, reading sci-fi novels, and doing your computer stuff."

"Computer stuff, he says." Jimmy looked at Bones and Jillian with a pained expression on his face. "I am unappreciated in my time." He sighed and took a stack of papers from the coffee table. "I can see you're in a hurry, so here's what I've got." He cleared his throat. "You asked me to find out anything I could about the Sons of the Republic, a journal belonging to Samuel Adams, and the phrase 'Gates of Freedom' as it relates to Adams or Paul Revere."

Jimmy was dragging this out just to be annoying and Dane made a "hurry it up" gesture. Jimmy frowned at him over his glasses, cleared his throat again, louder this time, and continued.

"There's not much on the Sons of the Republic. They advocate for a second revolution-the usual stuff. The government took a look at them and decided they weren't a threat. I didn't get much on Gates of Freedom, either. The phrase only appears in personal correspondence, and its meaning is never explained. It's always as if the writer assumes the reader knows what he's talking about. What's interesting are the names of the letter writers and the recipients. Guys like Samuel Adams, John Hancock, William Mackay, Paul Revere, James Swann, and Joseph Warren."

"All members of the Sons of Liberty," Dane mused.

"And all from Boston," Jillian added.

"It seems the Gates of Freedom is something known only to the Boston branch of the Sons of Liberty. At least, I couldn't find the phrase among the writings of any other members, or any other patriots for that matter."

"How did you manage to review so much data in such a short time?" Bones asked, placing his glass on the coffee table.

"I used my computer to hack into the Library of Congress and some university libraries."

"How did you get your computer connected to theirs?"

"It's the Internet, my friend. It's a network of interconnected computers all around the world. One day soon, everybody will be hooked into it: businesses, institutions, even individuals. It's going to change everything."

"If you say so, Jimmy." Dane had learned long ago not to get Jimmy started predicting the future. The guy had seen too many movies. "What else do you have?"

"Nothing definitive, but I think the Boston branch of the Sons of Liberty had a secret headquarters. Everybody knows they held secret meetings in various locations, but I think they might have also had a permanent meeting place for the most important stuff. I found an excerpt of a letter from Thomas Young to Paul Revere containing the phrase, "meet behind the Gates of Freedom.""

"And the journal?" Jillian asked.

"That one was tricky. If you want John Adams' journal, that's easy to find. Sam's, not so much. In fact, the only reference I found was the story of something he said on his deathbed. A slave overheard it, and the tale was passed down through her family. According to her, a few days before his death, she came into his room to empty his chamber pot. They were alone, and he whispered her name. It was one of his rare moments of lucidity, so she hurried to his bedside. He grabbed hold of her with surprising strength and said, "Journal. The secret. Trumbull preserved."

"John Trumbull? The portrait artist?" Dane frowned. John Trumbull was a painter best known for his Revolutionary War portraits, particularly his Declaration of Independence painting. "If he preserved the secret, it must have been in a painting."

"There is a Trumbull portrait of Adams inside Faneuil Hall," Jillian offered. "It was painted shortly before his death."

"I suppose we could wait until the place opens and check it out, but I'd rather not. I'd like to stay ahead of the Sons of the Republic, just in case they're on our trail." Dane turned to Jillian. "You don't happen to have another secret passageway up your sleeve?"

"Don't worry about it." Jimmy handed him a sheet of paper. "I'm way ahead of you."

Dane looked at it and smiled.

"Jimmy, I owe you another bottle of scotch."

"What is it?" Bones asked.

"A warren of old tunnels runs beneath the Freedom Trail. Most are dead-ends, running only a few meters before reaching points where the ceiling has collapsed, sealing it off from the rest of the passageways. One stretch, however, is intact, and it runs right beneath Faneuil Hall. At least, it was when the trail markers were installed on the Freedom Trail."

"It will get us inside?"

"It will, according to the source I found. It's a secret a few blue hairs from the Paul Revere Heritage group were trying to keep to themselves."

"How do we get in?" Bones brimmed with pent-up energy, tapping his feet and drumming his fingers.

"The markers along the Freedom Trail all look the same: a ring of oak leaves encircling the words *The Freedom Trail-Boston* and this symbol in the middle." He tapped an image on the paper Dane held. "In one spot, the marker covers a manhole leading down into the passageway."

"Where?" Jillian had half-risen from her chair.

"That, I couldn't find out, but there's a subtle difference in that particular marker. If you look closely, it has lines like this on it." He indicated a second image, and Dane held it up so Bones and Jillian could get a better look.

"The crossed circle," Jillian breathed. She sprang from her seat and hugged Jimmy, who gave her an awkward pat on the back. "Thank you."

"No problem."

"All right, ladies and gentlemen." Bones stood, his eyes brimming with eagerness. "Let's find a creepy old tunnel."

CHAPTER 13

"So," Jillian said, "now we take a tour of the Freedom Trail, right?"

Dane adjusted the backpack in which he carried one of the lanterns. Jillian carried the other in her own pack. "Yep, let's start with Faneuil Hall."

"It's this way," she replied, turning and walking toward the right-hand side of City Hall.

Without looking both ways, they crossed Congress Street at a trot, not worrying about cars smashing into them at quarter past three in the morning. They entered the plaza and made a beeline for the historic building.

"Think the doors are locked?" Bones asked.

"More than likely." Jillian looked the building up and down. "And I wouldn't consider breaking any windows, either: this is the most heavily secure historic building in the city. The cops would be on us so fast that we wouldn't be able to blink. We need Jimmy's secret passageway."

"Here's the marker." Dane flicked on his Maglite and shone it on the gleaming disc. "No crossed circle. Where do you want to try next?"

Jillian pulled out her father's map of the Freedom Trail and unfolded it. "Give me some light." She ran her finger along the red line to the next stop. "Paul Revere's House."

They headed down narrow, cobblestoned Marshall Street and past the Hand Tavern, which Jillian told them had opened in 1765 and claimed to be the oldest tavern in America, standing dark on the left-hand side. The winding red line took them through the garlic-scented air of the North End.

"We're in North Square Park," Jillian said. "The Revere House is over here."

Here, the red-bricked path was outlined in gray, marking the trail. The bricks rose up into a wall bisected by a gray hexagonal building with a pitched roof. They passed through a swinging gate and inspected the Revere House up close.

The remains of the house were flush against the tall brick building adjacent to it. The uneven brick surface of the courtyard surrounded a wood-and-glass case that held a bronze bell. A wrought iron staircase hung off the back side of the house, and flower gardens sprung up here and there, offsetting the monotonous red with greens, whites and yellows, all washed out in the pale moonlight.

Dane kept the flashlight moving until he found the marker. No cross. The tunnel wasn't here.

"What's next?" he asked.

"What do you mean?" Bones sounded incredulous. "We walked all that way for a five-second scan?"

"There's nothing here." Dane indicated the marker.

"All right, let's move along." Bones turned and headed for the exits.

"A little brusque. Is he okay?" Jillian asked.

"I'm sure he is. He's obviously serious about solving this mystery. I don't think I've ever seen him so focused on something that wasn't a combat situation."

They caught up with Bones just outside the gate.

"Which way?" Bones asked.

They followed the long bricked pathway past stately oaks that looked old enough to have witnessed the first shots of the Revolution. They came to a halt in front of a tall, dark shape. Dane moved his flashlight about until it came to rest on a long face.

"I think I know what this is." Bones brought his own light to bear.

A fifteen-foot-high statue with a smooth granite base loomed before them-- Paul Revere mounted on his horse. They stared at the statue for several moments. There was dignity in Revere's face, and a sense of the gravity of the task he undertook on that cold April night. Dane felt a touch of that same feeling. Here they were, three ordinary people on a mission, much like the one Revere undertook when he kicked his horse into motion and sent him speeding across the Charles River toward Lexington and Concord. Dane reached out and ran his fingers across the cool, granite surface, transfixed by the moment.

"Hey, Maddock, I think I found the marker."

That got Dane's attention. He joined Bones, who

knelt a few feet away from the statue. Sure enough, they could just make out the cross pattern behind the ornate engravings.

"This has to be it." He and Bones put down their lights and set to work. Dane strained with the effort, every muscle in his arms, back, and neck tensed as he poured all of his strength into working the cover loose until, finally, it broke free. They slid the metal disc aside and shone their lights into the hole, revealing rusted iron rungs descending to a brick passageway.

Dane tested the weight of the first rung, found it to be solid, and led the way down. Jillian followed, and then Bones climbed in, pausing to replace the marker over the hole before climbing the rest of the way down. Taking a moment to get their bearings, they set off in a Southwesterly direction.

"By car, it's a little over half-a mile to Faneuil Hall," Jillian said, "but if this tunnel is a straight shot, it should be even less."

Dane resisted the urge to jog, even run. All around them were signs that time was catching up to this passageway: missing bricks, leaning walls, sagging sections of ceiling, and collapsed side tunnels.

"Nobody sneeze." Bones echoed Dane's thoughts. "I don't want to end up like the Wicked Witch."

They paused at the first side passage that had not collapsed.

"What do you think?" Dane shone his light into the darkness. "Based on how fast we've been walking, I'd say we're a little less than half a mile."

"Let's check it out." Bones took the lead, still

eyeing the ceiling suspiciously.

The tunnel ended at a set of crumbling stone steps. Dane mounted them with trepidation, and felt the mortar crunch under his feet with every step. They stopped in front of a heavy wooden door on iron hinges. He took hold of the knob and took a deep breath.

"Here goes nothing." He turned the knob and pulled. The door gave an inch, then, with a loud crack, broke free of its hinges. Dane suddenly found himself holding up a six foot tall door. "Here." He handed it to Bones. "Find something to do with this."

The doorway opened into a dusty crawlspace, its floor cluttered with broken crates and moldering burlap bags. At the far end, a smaller, sturdier door led to a little-used storage room. From there, they mounted a staircase that led up to the main floor.

"This is it," Jillian whispered. "The Great Hall of Peter Faneuil's marketplace. Better known as Faneuil Hall."

Dane directed his beam out into the room and started when he saw George Washington staring back at him.

"Why, hello General. Fancy meeting you here." Bones strode into the room and gave the bust of America's first president a noogie.

Washington's wasn't the only sculpture in the hall. Looking at the alcoves set in the baby blue walls, Dane recognized John Quincy Adams, Frederick Douglas, Lucy Stone, Daniel Webster, and Samuel Adams. Moving past them, he played his light across the walls, scanning the portraits that hung in gilded frames.

"Anybody see Adams? We've got to make this quick. The last thing we need is for someone to drive by and see our lights through the window."

"Here he is!" Jillian's voice trembled with excitement, pointing to a spot behind where Dane stood.

Dane turned and looked. The statesman, clad all in red, stood before a bookcase. He clutched a sheaf of papers and seemed to look down on them with a hint of disapproval.

"He looks more laid-back on the beer bottles," Bones observed.

"That's because it's not Sam Adams on the beer; it's Paul Revere." Dane saw the confused expression on Bones' face and went on. "They were originally going to call it Paul Revere Beer, but the name Sam Adams tested better with consumers. They'd already designed the label and, as you pointed out, Paul Revere's is a friendlier face. So, there you have it."

"That's jacked-up. I'm going to write somebody a letter when we get back to base. I've been drinking under false pretenses."

"How about we look for the hidden message and argue about beer labels later?" Jillian moved in close and scrutinized the portrait. "Looks like a regular painting to me."

"Maybe on the back?" Bones tipped the bottom of the painting and peered behind it. "Nothing."

"Hold on a minute." Dane moved two steps closer and cocked his head. "There's something there."

Bones and Jillian moved back to stand beside him.

"I don't see anything." Bones scratched his chin.

"Most of the individual portraits from this time period have dull backgrounds—usually shades of a single color, but not this one. Look at the spine of each book. It's subtle, but it's there."

After a moment's pause, Jillian and Bones spoke on top of one another.

"I see it!"

"Whoa, dude!"

"Each spine has one of the symbols from our list. Jillian, you've got the key?"

She reached into her backpack and took out a notebook in which she'd copied down the key to the cipher: letters and numbers in one column, the corresponding symbols in the other. "I'm going to need a minute to figure this out. You guys keep an eye on the street."

Dane and Bones extinguished their lights and moved to either side of the hall. The floor-to-ceiling windows provided a clear view of the street. His heart pounding out a rhythmic beat and cold sweat dripping down his neck, Dane peered up and down the street while Jillian puzzled out the clue in the painting. Twice, she had to hurriedly douse her light when Dane spotted headlights in the distance. A police car approached. That was not what they needed right now.

Finally, after what felt like hours, Jillian cried out in triumph. "I've got it!"

"What does it say?" Dane hurried over to see what she had written.

"The secret lies with the five martyrs."

"Oh, that helps." Bones exhaled sharply. "History's filled with martyrs, and we have to figure out which five he gave chunks of his journal to?"

"This is Boston," Jillian said. "And we're talking about the American Revolution."

"Hold on." Dane's momentary disappointment had vanished, replaced by an almost manic excitement. "Aren't the five victims of the Boston Massacre buried together?"

"Yes!" Jillian nodded vigorously. "And the grave is right here on the Freedom Trail!"

"I think we'd better find it quick." Bones stared out the window. "Because I think somebody just spotted us."

They followed his line of sight and spotted the same police officer who had questioned Dane and Bones after Andrews' accident. He strode along Congress Street toward Faneuil Hall, his eyes locked on the window where Dane and his friends stood.

"O'Meara," Dane breathed. "Let's get out of here."

CHAPTER 14

They hurried back through the basement area and down into the underground passageway. Dane felt confident that O'Meara, if he had even seen them, had no chance of finding them down here. By the time they made their way back to the entrance at the foot of the Revere Monument, however, he had a new worry.

"What happens if he sees us climbing out of the passageway? We don't know where he's patrolling."

"We'll have to risk it," Bones said. "I'll go first. If he sees me, I'll draw him off. I can outrun him no problem."

"Are you sure?" A few days ago, Dane wouldn't have cared if Bones got himself arrested or not, but now he realized he'd come to like the guy, and even rely on his solid presence. "Maxie won't like it if you get arrested."

"It wouldn't be the first time I've run from the cops. I'll lose him and meet you two at the graveyard. Where is it?"

"The Granary Burying Ground. Unfortunately, it's

a mile or so back the way we came. We'll have to take the roundabout way and hope we don't meet up with O'Meara."

As they made their way toward the burying ground, Jillian filled them in on its history. Founded in 1660, the Granary Burying Ground was the final resting place of many notable patriots, including Paul Revere, three signers of the Declaration of Independence, and the victims of the Boston Massacre.

As they passed beneath the imposing gateway, Dane recognized the sturdy columns and large, ornate entablature as Egyptian Revival architecture. He noted the winged hourglasses carved into it, as well as the many skeletons and winged skulls engraved in the weathered headstones. He looked at the macabre images and felt as if he'd been transported to another time and place. Strange, such a creepy old cemetery would be located in the middle of a bustling, modern city.

They wound through the silent cemetery, keeping an eye out for O'Meara, or any other unwelcome observers, until Jillian called them to a halt.

"The grave is right here." She looked around, making sure they were alone, then flicked on her light.

Dane had expected an elaborate tomb, but only a simple headstone marked the victims' resting place. It read:

The Remains of
SAMUEL GRAY
SAMUEL MAVERICK

JAMES CALDWELL
CRISPUS ATTUCKS
and
PATRICK CARR
Victims of the Boston Massacre
March 5, 1770

"I thought it would be bigger," Bones said. "What now? Find a shovel and start digging?"

"I don't know." Dane circled the grave marker, looking it over, and then shone his light across the ground. "Wait! Check this out." His light shone on an old foot marker. Unlike its counterparts on the surrounding graves, this one was large, with a thick, brass plaque attached to the weathered stone. It bore no writing, only single image.

"It's the crossed circle again!" Jillian whispered. "I think this is it!"

Dane thought so too, but didn't want to jinx them by saying so.

"Listen, how about you two find a place out of sight to wait for me? Three people with flashlights, huddled around a grave in the middle of the night could draw attention. Give me a minute to get my night vision back and I'll be good to go."

Jillian started to protest, but Bones took her by the elbow and steered her away into the darkness.

Dane took out his Swiss army knife and set to work on the screws that held the plaque in place. They didn't budge. More than two centuries of exposure to the elements had frozen them solid. He tried prying the plaque loose with one of his knife blades. It gave a little—enough for him to see a hollowed-out space behind it. Encouraged, he kept working, but made no further progress. Minutes flew and Dane grew increasingly frustrated. Finally, in a fit of pique, he ran to the nearby fence, wrenched off one of the ornamental top spikes, wedged it beneath the edge of the plate, and used a rock to hammer it in until the plate broke free.

"What the hell are you doing?" Bones called softly. "Trying to wake the dead?"

"I had to. I'm done now."

"Hurry up. With our luck, O'Meara's right around the corner."

Cupping his Maglite to hide its beam, Dane shone it into the hollowed-out section of the foot stone, revealing a hinged, metal door with four numbered tumblers. A Colonial combination lock!

Dane bit his lip. What four digit number might work? He thought of the headstone and tried 1705. No joy. He racked his brain for any dates that made sense: Samuel Adams death in 1803, Lexington and Concord in 1775. Neither worked.

He checked his watch. In a few hours, the streets would begin filling with people celebrating Independence Day. Time was almost up.

Independence Day! That was it. He chuckled and turned the fourth tumbler.

1776

This time, the door swung open and he reached inside and withdrew a small bundle wrapped in oilcloth, and unwrapped it to reveal a thin rectangle encased in a leather cover. The cover was, in itself, a work of art: the Liberty Tree, Faneuil Hall, and the Old North Church were stamped into its surface. An ornate band ringed the edges. He opened the cover and something slid out and fell to the ground. He tucked the cover into his backpack and picked up the fallen object: a small book bound in plain leather, the pages inside yellow and brittle with age. The inscription on the first page read:

The Journal of Samuel Adams.

Eager to see what was written inside, he moved into the shadow of an elm tree, flicked on his light, and held it in his teeth and carefully turned the pages. He saw nothing that resembled a clue. The pages were filled with Adams' thoughts on freedom and liberty, but nothing that resembled a code, and certainly no hint of any secrets. He frowned. He had a sense that he was missing something obvious, but what? Invisible ink?

"Maddock!" Bones whispered.

Dane raised his head just in time for a bright, white light to blind him.

"It's you. Step out here and keep your hands where I can see them."

Shielding his eyes, Dane moved toward the sound of O'Meara's voice. "I can explain." In fact, he couldn't explain. At least, not if he planned on lying, which he absolutely intended to do.

"Do I really need to tell you that grave robbing is a

crime?" O'Meara lowered his light and Dane squeezed his eyelids closed and tried to shake away the bright spots that filled his vision.

"I wasn't robbing a grave. I'm doing research."

"I don't have time for your lies. Give me Adams' journal and I'll let you go."

"Did you say Adams' journal?" Dane couldn't believe it.

"Try playing games with me and I'll shoot you for resisting arrest." O'Meara took a step closer, still holding his revolver steady. "Give me the journal."

"How did you know?" Sudden understanding struck him. "You're a Son of the Republic."

"Not as dumb as you look. I appreciate you being our bloodhound, but your usefulness is at an end. I'm not going to tell you again. Give me the journal." He leveled his service revolver at Dane's midsection.

Dane considered his options. Running was not a good idea. At this distance, O'Meara would have to be a lousy shot to miss, and he stood too far away for Dane to try wresting the weapon from his grasp.

"Fine." Dan closed the book, sighed, and tossed it in a high arc.

As the book flew through the air, two things happened: someone cried out in the darkness and, as O'Meara turned toward the sound, a rock struck him on the forehead. He crumpled to the ground, clutching his head.

Dane took off, weaving through the maze of gravestones and crypts, following the sound of pounding feet that he knew to be Bones and Jillian. He caught up with them quickly, and they ran together until they reached the Benjamin Franklin statue far along the Freedom Trail. Fresh off the first stage of SEAL training, the run took no toll on Dane or Bones, but Jillian was gassed. She stood, hands on knees, gasping for breath.

"You think he's coming after us?" Bones asked, looking out into the darkness.

"If he does, it won't be on foot. He'd never catch up with us, assuming you didn't give him a concussion. In any case, he has no reason to follow us now. I gave him the journal."

"You did what?" Jillian panted. "We have to go back. You can't let him have it." She started to head back in the direction they had come, but Dane stopped her with four words.

"We don't need it."

Jillian froze and turned slowly around, stray locks of hair plastered to her glistening forehead. "What do you mean?"

"I'll show you."

They huddled in the shelter of the dense shrubbery by Old City Hall, and Dane took out the leather cover.

"There was nothing in the journal, but look at what it was wrapped in. I didn't realize what I was looking at, but it struck me right about the time O'Meara asked for the journal." He shone his light on the symbols around the edge of the leather rectangle. "Look familiar?"

"The symbols from the key! So the journal itself

was a red herring. Nice job, Maddock." Bones gave Dane an enthusiastic fist bump. "Some of these are pretty worn out, though. Do you we'll be able to translate them?'

"I've got a plan. Jillian, lend me your notebook and pencil." He tore out a sheet of paper, laid it over the leather square, and began lightly rubbing the edge of the pencil lead over the paper. Soon, the symbols appeared.

"My partner knows his stuff." Bones' voice held a note of pride.

"Partner?" Dane raised an eyebrow and passed the sheet to Jillian for translation.

"You prefer amigo, maybe? Kemosabe? Soul sister?"

"Partner is fine."

In two minutes, Jillian had a translation. "It's sort of a poem."

Beneath the twin beacons.
That kindled liberty.
Behind the Gates of Freedom.
The Father and his words.

"Um. Okay." Bones scratched his head. "Is this, like, about God? You know, the Father?"

"I don't think so." Dane mulled it over. "Remember, the Sons of the Republic are looking for Washington's Prophecy."

"Yes!" Jillian's eyes gleamed with excitement. "Even in his lifetime, George Washington was known as the 'Father of His Country.' Adams would certainly have been familiar with that title, and would likely have used it."

"You're right. That should have been obvious. My bad." Bones took the poem from Jillian and looked it over. "If I'm not mistaken, we've got the 'twin beacons that kindled liberty' right here in our backpacks. Now we need to figure out what the 'beneath' part means."

Dane looked at Jillian and could tell they were thinking the same thing.

"I know exactly where we need to go."

CHAPTER 15

Dane gazed up at the steeple of the Old North Church. Fitting that the search would end here at this 270 year-old house of worship where, in 1775, sexton Robert Newman hung two lanterns, thus warning the Charlestown patriots of the movements of British forces.

"One if by land, two if by sea," he whispered.

"Talking to yourself?"

Dane jerked his head about, startled by Bones' sudden appearance. "How did you manage to sneak up on me like that?" Dane prided himself on his acute hearing and vision, and sharp instincts. Seldom could someone do to him what Bones had just done.

"I'm your worst nightmare: a SEAL-trained Indian. You ought to see me up in the mountains. Of course, that's impossible."

"Do you see Jillian anywhere?"

"She should be here any minute. I kept an eye on her most of the way, but don't let her know that. She looked so proud of herself, getting all sneaky."

They had split up before making their way back up the Freedom Trail to the church, figuring they stood a better chance of eluding O'Meara that way. Dane hoped the police officer and Son of the Republic had gone to work on deciphering the journal, and would leave them in peace, at least long enough for them to find the Gates of Freedom and whatever lay beyond them. He caught a glimpse of a shadow moving toward them, and relaxed. Jillian had made it.

"Here she comes," Bones whispered.

"I see her."

"Maglites on three. One... two..."

On three, they spun and shone their lights in Jillian's face.

"Fine, I suck at sneaking. Now turn those things off."

"So, how do we get in?" Dane asked. "Bones, could you pick the lock?"

"Probably, but I'll bet the door is alarmed. Let me take a quick look around."

They circled the old church, Bones scrutinizing every window. Finally, when they reached the back, he stopped. "I don't see alarms on any of these windows. I hate to do it, but I think our best bet is to pop out one of the small panes of glass," he indicated the window just to the right of the back door, "and raise the sash."

"Do it quietly." Dane looked around, still expecting O'Meara to appear at any moment. He watched as Bones took out a handkerchief, wrapped it around his hand, and knocked out the pane above the window latch. The tinkling of shattering glass sounded like gunfire in the quiet night. Still using the handkerchief to cover his hands, Bones reached inside, opened the latch, and forced the window upward. It rose with a shrill squeak, and Dane stole a glance around the side of the building to see if anyone was on the street, but they were still alone. So far, so good.

Minutes later, they were inside the church. Bones closed the window, expressing regret that, if he'd only had the proper tools, he could have removed the glass without shattering it.

"How many burglaries did you commit when you were a kid?" Jillian asked.

"More than seven, less than a thousand. That's all you need to know."

"So, where do we begin our search?" Dane asked Jillian. "Downstairs, I assume."

"Most people don't realize there's a crypt beneath Old North Church. Thirty-seven tombs and over a thousand bodies. I think it will be down there."

She led the way into the basement. They descended a winding, narrow staircase, their footsteps echoing loudly off the wooden steps. At the bottom, a door on the left opened into the crypt.

Here, the walls were rough brick, some tombs sealed with doors of wood or slate, others covered in plaster. Above them were gray slate nameplates memorializing those entombed beneath the historical church.

"What are we looking for?" Bones whispered.

"Anything that catches your eye. The crossed circle, something related to the Sons of Liberty. Go with your gut."

As they moved through the crypt, the weight of

history seemed to settle on Dane. His eyes passed across name after name, the dates driving home the significance of this place. The longer they searched, however, the less hopeful he felt.

"It *has* to be here," Jillian whispered.

"Keep looking." His voice rang hollow. The dark, twisting passageway ended up ahead, and nothing looked promising.

Bones held his light up to the nameplate above the last tomb. "Here lies Culper Ring. That's a weird name. No birth and death dates." He turned back to face Dane and Jillian. "Guess we've hit a dead end."

"I don't think so." Dane brushed past Bones and began a careful examination of the tomb and the surrounding wall.

"What do you mean?" Jillian's hopeful voice held a measure of doubt, as if reluctant to believe they hadn't failed.

"It's not a person's name. The Culper Ring was one of George Washington's spy rings during the war."

"You're sure it's not just a coincidence?" Bones asked.

"Nope, but I've got a feeling." He lowered the beam of his light to the floor and his heart leapt. "Now I'm sure."

On either side of the tomb, shallow indentations in the shape of the lantern bases were carved in the stone. Metal bands formed the lines of the cross.

"That's got to be where the lanterns go!" Bones exclaimed.

Dane and Jillian removed the lanterns from their

backpacks and carefully set them in place.

"Any day now," Bones muttered.

The tomb remained sealed.

Dane tried switching the lanterns, then turning them as if they were keys, but met with no success. He removed one and touched the recessed area in the floor. The metal bands seemed out of place. The crossed circle could have been carved into the stone, so why the metal? He ran a finger across the smooth, cold surface of one strip.

Cold!

Inspiration struck in a flash. Could it be?

"Maybe the lanterns need to be lit!"

"If they do, we're screwed," Bones said. "I doubt there's still oil in these babies after two hundred years."

Dane cursed and pounded his fist into his open palm. Could they escape unseen, find a store open and selling lamp oil on Independence Day, and sneak back down here without getting caught or once again running afoul of the Sons of the Republic? Would their quest be thwarted by something so mundane?

"Actually, we're good to go." Jillian pulled a small can out of her pack and handed it to Dane. "I know it's dumb, but I thought it would be cool to explore the Gates of Freedom using Paul Revere's lanterns, so I replaced the wicks and brought a little lamp oil." "You might have saved the day." In short order, he had filled the lanterns. Jillian offered him a disposable lighter, but Bones objected.

"Put that crap away." He produced a Zippo and handed it to Dane. "Only the best."

"I've never seen you smoke."

"I don't. I just think Zippos are cool. You can't deny it came in handy."

"True. Now, let's see if I'm right." Dane set the lanterns back in place, lit the first, then held his breath and lit the second. He was out of ideas. If this didn't work...

He hadn't needed to worry. The lanterns blazed brightly and, with a hollow clack, the doorway to the arched tomb slid sideways into the wall.

"Yes!" Bones raised his arms in exultation. "You are the man!"

Stale, damp air wafted forth, causing the lanterns to flicker. Dane shone his Maglite through the opening, revealing a downward sloping tunnel. The Liberty Tree was engraved in the stone floor beneath the words, *The Gates of Freedom.*

Here was the passage they had sought-- the hidden entrance to the secret headquarters of the Sons of Liberty.

"Let's move, Maddock. Think we should take the lanterns with us?"

"I do. Maybe we can find something to wedge the door open, though. We don't want to be trapped inside.

Bones pried a few of the loose bricks out of the wall and set them in place.

"All right." Dane handed one lantern to Bones and hefted the other. "Let's see where she leads." Heart racing, he took a step inside.

A sense of exhilaration surged through him at the

knowledge that he followed a path no one alive had taken. He felt the same heady sensation that came over him whenever he dove on a sunken ship, or into an underwater cave, but more intense.

Behind them the door began to slide back into place until, with a loud thump, it ground to a halt halfway across.

"I wonder if it's still under warranty?" Bones mused. "I guess we didn't need to wedge it open after all."

Dane led the way down into the darkness. Bones' and Jillian's footsteps echoed, one heavy, one light, as they followed. Constructed of the same brick as the crypt, the tunnel peaked in an arch about six feet high—just enough clearance for Dane to pass without ducking. Bones wasn't so fortunate, and he complained vociferously as they descended.

"Shut up, Bones. You're ruining the mood," Jillian scolded.

The tunnel curved to the left and then, straight ahead, ended at a set of double doors.

"Oh my God, we've found it." Jillian's voice trembled. She quickened her pace, hurrying past Dane.

"Stop!" Dane called, taking her by the arm and pulling her back.

"What's up?" Bones poked his head over Danes shoulder.

"Look." Dane raised his lantern high. Here, the sloping passage leveled out, and the walls and ceiling were perfectly square. Up above, a single, gray slab hung with no visible means of support. "I don't like the looks of this."

"A booby trap?" Bones sounded doubtful. "I think you've seen too many movies, Maddock."

"Why else would they square off just this part of the passageway, when everything else, even the doorway, is arched? And check that out."

He pointed to the floor, where the coppery scales and onyx eye of giant, segmented rattlesnake gleamed in the lamplight.

"Creepy." Bones shifted his weight from foot to foot, evidently discomfited by the sight. "Why use a chopped up snake? Some weird cult?"

"No, it's from Benjamin Franklin's *Join or Die* cartoon. It symbolized the need for the colonies to be united against the British."

"You think those are the steps?" Bones asked.

"The opposite, I believe. Do you remember your American history?"

"Don't Tread on Me." Jillian squeezed Dane's arm. "I think you're right."

"Fifty-fifty chance, then." Bones ran his fingers through his hair. "Is it really worth it? I mean, I want to see this through, but do we want to take the chance of getting squashed just to see this headquarters, or whatever is back there?"

"I'm going." Before they could stop her, Jillian stepped over the snake's rattle and onto the slate floor. She froze, looking up, but the ceiling held fast. "Come on, chickens," she called, carefully making her way to the other side.

Dane and Bones followed along. Bones' feet were

so large, and some of the places they could safely step were so small, that Dane worried they wouldn't make it across without a misstep, but Bones proved to be more than agile enough to safely navigate the passageway.

"It wasn't any worse than the obstacle courses we've run through in training." Bones saw the relief in Dane's eyes. "Quit worrying about me and open these doors."

Carved in the face of the two doors, the Liberty Tree spread its branches before them. Dane reached out and twisted the handles, and was pleased to find they turned easily. He pushed the doors open and damp air, heavy with the smell of mold, assaulted his nostrils.

Inside, a stone staircase led upward. Dane counted the risers—thirteen steps. Fitting. When he reached the top step, he froze, awestruck.

They had found the secret headquarters of the Sons of Liberty!

CHAPTER 16

"I can't believe we found it," Dane whispered. The lantern light shone on high, vaulted ceilings and cast shadows in the empty shelves that lined the walls on either side. Directly in front of them stood a long, wooden table, its surface coated with dust and mold. Chairs were scattered about, some broken. Lanterns identical to the ones he and Bones held hung from hooks in the corners, and a huge chandelier dangled from a chain in the room's center, the remains of candles still evident.

"I'll bet it was something to see in its day." Bones' eyes were filled with wonder. "Did anybody bring a camera?"

Neither Dane nor Jillian answered. Both were mesmerized by what lay at the far end of the room. As if in a trance, Dane crossed the floor, eyes locked on the fantastic sight.

Looking down upon them from atop a high pedestal sat George Washington. Rendered in white marble, the first President of the United States gazed serenely into the distance.

"This doesn't make sense." Jillian stared wide-eyed at the memorial. "Washington wasn't one of the Boston Sons of Liberty, and by the time he rose to prominence, the organization wouldn't have needed a secret headquarters. Why would they build a memorial to him down here?"

Dane tried to reply, but he couldn't speak. He had just read the inscription on the base of the pedestal.

Here lies
His Excellency, George Washington
Commander In-Chief of the Continental Army
First President of the United States
Father of His Country
February 22, 1732- July 4, 1791
May God Forgive Us

"What... what does this mean?" Jillian stammered.

"This is weird," Bones agreed.

They were right. Washington hadn't died in 1791. In fact, he'd served as president until 1797 and passed away in 1799. Dane gazed up at George Washington's face, as if understanding lay in those cold, stone eyes.

"What's this on the floor?" Bone asked.

Dane looked down. Beneath a layer of dust lay a bronze plaque. He knelt, brushed it clean, and read aloud.

"On July 4, 1791, His Excellency, George Washington, President of these United States, died as he had lived, in service to his country. Believing the bonds that unite our thirteen states too fragile to survive the news that the Father of our infant nation

had fallen to an assassin's bullet, we chose the honorable Charles Washington to serve in his stead. May God forgive us for our deception. It is our fervent prayer that, some day, the citizens of this great nation shall know the truth and understand that what we did, we did for our country."

"Who the hell is Charles Washington?" Bones asked.

"George Washington's brother." Dane racked his brain, trying to remember all he knew about Washington's family. "Charles was only a couple of years younger, but he..." Dane fell silent.

"He what?" Jillian's hands trembled as she shone her light on the plaque.

"He died in 1799, right around the same time as George."

"This is freaking crazy." Bones dropped to one knee alongside Dane and read the plaque again. "So Washington was assassinated in 1791? Why would they think the country couldn't handle it?"

Dane felt numb. The revelation did seem too crazy to be true, but here lay the proof. "Like it says here, the nation was fragile. There was strong sentiment that the thirteen colonies should be independently governed-- more of a loose alliance for mutual defense than a true nation. Washington was the most important symbol of our new country, and a strong force for unity. He was respected both in the North and the South. People trusted him; some practically worshiped him."

"So his brother stepped into his shoes as

president? How could he pull that off?" Bones sounded as shocked as Dane.

"It's not like they had television back then. How many people actually saw Washington up close, or saw him at all? And he was an old man by the standards of his day, and few men have gone through what he did. If someone noticed subtle differences in his appearance, they'd likely chalk it up to the ravages of time and the stress of his office. As long as he and Charles looked somewhat alike, and those in his inner circle were in on the deception, they could have gotten away with it."

"This isn't a monument," Bones said. "This is a tomb."

"Oh my God!" Jillian cried.

Dane and Bones sprang to their feet and looked up at the wall where the circle of light from her Maglite wavered. They had missed the words carved above the tomb.

The Last Words of His Excellency, George Washington

I heard a voice saying, `Son of the Republic, look and learn,' I beheld a dark, shadowy being, like an angel, floating in mid-air, between Europe and America. Dipping water out of the ocean in the hollow of each hand, he sprinkled some upon America with his right hand, while with his left hand he cast some on Europe. Immediately a cloud rose from these countries, and moved slowly westward, until it enveloped America in its murky folds. Sharp flashes of lightning gleamed through it at intervals, and I heard the smothered groans and cries of the

American people. I cast my eyes upon America, saw our beloved flag raised, and the cloud was driven back, and I beheld villages and towns and cities springing up one after another until the whole land from the Atlantic to the Pacific was dotted with them.

Again, I heard the voice say, `Son of the Republic, look and learn.' At this the dark shadowy angel turned his face southward, and from Africa I saw an ill omened specter approach our land and a dark cloud arose in the South. As I continued looking I saw a bright angel, on whose brow rested a crown of light, on which was traced the word `Union,' bearing the American flag which he placed between the divided nation, and said, `Remember ye are brethren.' Instantly, the inhabitants, casting from them their weapons united around the National Standard.

A third time, the voice said, `Son of the Republic, look and learn.' And now rose up, from within America itself, many people bearing a flag, and cloaked in zeal, and they cried "Return! Return!" And a dark cloud rose from their lips and blinded our eyes, so we could not see that theirs was a black flag, and they tore at the bonds that held us as one. But our flag pierced the black cloud, and the sun shone down, and once more I beheld the villages, towns and cities springing up where I had seen them before, while the bright angel, planting the standard he had brought in the midst of them, cried with a loud voice: `While the stars remain, and the heavens send down dew upon the earth, so long shall the Union last.'

July 4, 1791

"That's not the prophecy," Jillian snapped. "The

first trials are almost the same, but the last one is totally wrong." Quaking with rage, she backed away from the tomb.

"It's better," Dane said. "It sounds like the third trial is caused by false patriots, but they'll lose in the end."

"I guess we'll have to do something about that."

Dane whirled around. There, in the doorway, stood O'Meara.

CHAPTER 17

"We'll have to make sure nobody ever hears these words, or finds out this place even exists." O'Meara rounded the long meeting table, his revolver in one hand, a flashlight in the other. "Either one of you moves, you die. Now, put the lanterns down and your hands in the air. Nice and slow."

Dane complied, and Bones followed suit a moment later. He calculated the distance between himself and O'Meara, wondering if he could get to the officer before he fired, but the distance was too great. If Dane charged him, O'Meara would get off at least two shots. He might miss, but it wasn't likely. If the situation didn't improve, and quickly, Dane would have to risk it. His eyes darted to Jillian, who stood with her back to the wall. She clutched her backpack to her chest as if it might stop a bullet.

"Let her go." Dane knew his request was futile. The Sons of the Republic would want to keep this place, and the prophecy, a secret, and Jillian was a witness. They'd want to silence her.

O'Meara barked a laugh. "Are you kidding? She's one of us. You two were just too stupid to figure it out."

"The hell she is." Bones clenched his fists.

"How do you think I knew you were going to Old North Church?"

"She couldn't have gotten word to you, we were together..." Bones lapsed into shocked silence.

"Except for when we split up to go to the church." Dane looked at Jillian. "Is that why you fell behind?"

"I stopped at a pay phone and paged O'Meara." Her features relaxed and she sauntered over to stand beside the officer. "Where should we do it?" she asked O'Meara.

"Right here. We'll leave them down here, destroy the lanterns, and no one will ever find them."

Jillian gave them a speculative look. "Let's not get blood on Washington's tomb, though. That just seems disrespectful. How about over there?" She pointed to O'Meara's left.

O'Meara turned his head and a loud bang echoed through the chamber. O'Meara slumped to the ground, a gaping wound in the back of his head. Jillian stood looking down at him, a Beretta in her hand.

"Nice one." Bones nodded approvingly. "You had me believing you were on his side."

"I'm not on his side." Jillian turned her eyes back toward them. She looked different. Where there had been trepidation in her eyes, they now brimmed with confidence. "But I *am* a member of the Sons of the Republic." She raised the Beretta and aimed it at Dane.

"I paged O'Meara because he was a loose end I needed to tie up. Now it's time to sort you two out."

Dane grimaced. He wondered what exactly had been going through Jillian's mind the past two days.

"I don't get it," Bones said.

"What don't you get? My father was an enigma. He kept his research top-secret. Never told me a thing. So, when he was killed running away from O'Meara..."

"Wait! O'Meara killed your father?" Dane's stomach lurched. Andrews' own daughter.

"Technically, it was the car that killed him. You know, the one that ran him over. We wanted to find out who was helping him. O'Meara, being the idiot that he was, couldn't do as he was told and just follow my father to his meeting. He thought he could intimidate Dad into revealing what he knew. Dad ran for it."

"That's why O'Meara got to the scene so quickly." Anger boiled inside Dane. "You act like you don't even care. He was your father."

"Professor Nick Andrews wasn't much of a father." Jillian twisted her features into a dark scowl. "He cared only about his work. Everything else was an afterthought: me, my mother, his country. I ran away when I was sixteen and I've been on my own ever since. He's my only living relative and he never once looked for me. I only returned to my father's house because I needed his knowledge. The Sons of the Republic are my family now."

"Some family," Bones scoffed.

"You don't know anything about it. It's my cause. It's who I am. The rest of the world doesn't know me and doesn't care about me. I'm a phantom. I'm the crazy cat lady who moves every time her lease expires, never puts down roots, and spends all her time at the library. I don't think anyone outside the Sons even knows my name."

"If you're such a loner, why did you involve us?" Dane looked into her eyes and wondered how he'd ever found her attractive.

"You came to me, remember? I was going through his things and wasn't getting anywhere. You'd spoken to Remillard, so you were already ahead of me. Plus, you were a little extra muscle. A meat shield against the other members of my organization."

Dane considered this. "When those guys came after us out in front of Faneuil Hall, you didn't recognize them because they had come to the house; you knew them as members of the Sons of the Republic."

Her predatory grin was all the answer he needed.

"That's also why you were so eager to let Drinkel go. You were afraid he'd break down and tell the authorities about your little game." Dane kept a close eye on the Beretta. Jillian held it steady, her finger ready on the trigger. He needed a distraction.

"What's up with you people" Bones subtly shifted his weight. Dane could tell he was about to do something reckless. "Aren't you guys on the same side?"

"In the big picture, yes, but those of us who wish to lead are... competitive. Only the strongest survive. I wanted to be the one to deliver the true prophecy.

Instead, I'll be the one who discovered and dealt with the threat it posed. Either way..."

"Either way, you're a psychotic freak." Bones leapt toward Jillian, who whirled the gun in his direction.

Dane acted instantly. One of the lanterns still lay at his feet, and he kicked it at her with all his might. He'd played a little soccer as a kid and studied a lot of martial arts over the years, and it flew true—a burning missile hurtling toward her head.

Jillian flinched and pulled the trigger, but Bones moved too quickly for her. The bullet missed him. He rolled into Jillian's legs and she stumbled, giving Dane the opening he needed.

With a quickness borne of intense training and mind-numbing repetition, he grabbed her wrist in a vise grip, forcing her gun hand up and away from him and Bones. Screaming with impotent rage, she clawed at his face with her free hand and pulled the trigger of her Beretta again and again, sending a harmless fusillade of lead into the ceiling. When her magazine ran dry, she clicked the trigger a few more times, then released the Beretta and began raining punches on Dane's head and chest. Dane yanked her toward him, spun her about, and pinned her elbows together behind her back.

"Calm down," he snapped. "I'm not going to hit you, but I won't let you hit me either."

Her screams grew louder as she thrashed about. She stamped on his foot, then threw her head back, cracking him across the nose, which still pained him.

"Seriously?" He winced as hot pain lanced through him, but he held on.

A gunshot rang out and Jillian fell silent. Bones had retrieved O'Meara's weapon and fired a warning shot.

"Enough!" Illuminated by flickering lantern light, Bones loomed over Jillian, looking every inch of his nearly six and-a-half feet. Dane had to admit it made for an imposing sight. "I won't hit a woman either, but if you don't chill, I'll turn you over my knee. And I promise you won't like it."

Jillian no longer screamed, but her breath came in gasps and she shook like a palm frond in a hurricane. "You're going to tell the world about this place, aren't you?" she panted.

"Of course we are." Dane couldn't believe she would want to hide such a thing. "It's part of our history. People should know the truth."

"You can't. Washington is too important. So are the Sons of Liberty. You'll besmirch their memories. People already lack faith in America. This news would be a terrible blow." She still trembled, and Dane felt cold sweat trickle down her arms.

Bones brushed her concerns away. "People will just have to get over it."

"And what are you going to do to me?" Her voice had fallen to a mere whimper.

"We're going to turn you in to the police. They can't all be corrupt." Dane looked at O'Meara's fallen form.

"I'll tell them I'm the victim. You brought me down here and O'Meara tried to save me."

"The bullet that killed him came from the Beretta.

You know, the gun that only has your prints on it. Then there's the gunshot residue, and the testimony of two service men with exemplary records."

"Well, not quite exemplary," Bones added.

The last of Jillian's resistance crumbled. Her legs wobbled and she fell to the floor with a whimper, her sweat-slick arms slipping from Dane's grasp.

"Got anything we can use to bind her wrists?" Dane asked, looking around.

"Do we really need it? I think she's played out." They looked down at the young woman, who sat with her head buried in her hands, sobbing.

"Let's get her out of here," Dane said.

Without warning, Jillian lashed out at the one remaining lantern that still burned only feet from her. With a metallic clang and the sound of breaking glass, the room was plunged into darkness. Footsteps echoed through the room as Jillian fled. Chasing the sound of her footfalls, Dane dug the Maglite out of his pocket and flicked it on to see her stumble over a fallen chair.

Dane closed the distance, but Jillian reached the stairs first and hurtled down them.

"Jillian!" he shouted. "Don't!"

At the foot of the steps, Jillian looked back over her shoulder as she ran, and he saw the panic in her eyes. He could tell she was thinking of nothing but escape.

"The snake!" he cried, but Jillian didn't seem to hear.

She plunged through the double doors and stepped directly onto the rattlesnake's head, which sank into the bedrock, causing her to lose her footing. Jillian cried out in surprise as she fell, but her cry turned to a scream of pure terror as a solid block of stone came crashing down on top of her.

The boom of falling stone reverberated through the chamber and the impact rocked the floor. Dane wobbled and felt Bones put a steadying hand on his shoulder.

"Is she..." Bones didn't finish the question.

"Yes. I saw it happen."

"And now we're blocked in."

Dane shone his light all around the chamber, looking for another way out, but all he saw were cracks in the ceiling.

Cracks that hadn't been there before, radiating out from above the stairwell, and expanding. The first chunk of ceiling came crashing down, exploding at their feet and spraying them in a shower of rock and mortar.

"I think we've got another problem."

CHAPTER 18

The falling ceiling chased Dane and Bones the length of the meeting hall. Their lights bobbed in front of them, slicing through the dusty air. Dane searched frantically for an escape route.

"There has to be another way out!" he shouted over the din. "They wouldn't want to be stuck in here if someone triggered the booby trap!" He winced as a chunk of falling stone the size of his head smashed a chair into sawdust.

"Any ideas where?" Bones called.

"Have you seen the crossed circle anywhere?" He dodged to his right to avoid being crushed by more falling debris.

"I have! On the tomb. Grab the lanterns." Bones left Dane behind, his long legs eating up the distance between them and Washington's tomb. He scooped up one of the fallen lanterns and dashed ahead.

Dane grabbed the other, hoping against hope that Bones was right. He hadn't noticed any crossed circles on the tomb.

"Up here!" Bones pointed to the top of the pedestal. "There's an indentation on each corner, just like the ones at the entrance."

Although the world crashed down around him, Dane managed a smile. Bones was just tall enough to see over the top of the pedestal. "Guess I need to keep you around," Dane shouted and felt for the indentation. Finding it, he slid the lantern home.

"I'm also good for reaching things on high shelves. Still got my Zippo?"

Dane fished the lighter out of his pocket and, praying that all the kicking around hadn't destroyed the lanterns, lit the wicks.

It seemed the chamber would surely collapse on them long before the passageway opened. They stood there in the dust-choked air, shielding their heads from falling debris. He looked back and saw what looked like a wall of stone creeping toward them. They had only seconds.

And then the face of the tomb slid open. Dane and Bones squeezed inside, grateful to be out of immediate danger.

"See a way out?" Dane asked.

"All I see is a coffin."

Despite the peril, Dane couldn't help but pause to look at Washington's final resting place. He'd been to Mount Vernon and visited Washington's tomb, but now he knew the truth. He and Bones were the only living men to see the true tomb of the father of their country. It both thrilled and saddened him.

"Maddock! Back there." Bones trained his light on the far end of the tomb, where a trapdoor had opened. They crawled through and found themselves in a tunnel twin to the one through which they had entered the meeting hall.

Dane regained his feet and sprinted up the passageway. The sound of the collapsing room faded as they climbed higher, racing toward freedom. They rounded a turn and came to a sudden halt.

A heap of rubble barred their way. That had run directly into one of the many passages that had collapsed decades, maybe centuries ago.

"Now what?" Dane couldn't believe they'd escaped with their lives, only to have their way barred.

"We can't go back. The ceiling came down over the trapdoor we came through. The only way is forward."

Dane sighed. "We'd better roll up our sleeves and get to work."

Holding their Maglites in their teeth, they set to clearing the rubble. They worked in silence, sweat and dust coating them from head to foot. It seemed a Sisyphean task. Every stone they cleared revealed only more rubble, but neither spoke of giving up.

While they labored, Dane reflected on the whirlwind events of the past few days. He realized that, though he and Bones certainly had their differences, they were shallow, superficial things. Bones had no reason to join Dane on this crazy adventure, and could have abandoned the chase at any point. But no matter the danger, his resolve had never wavered. And now, faced with a seemingly hopeless situation, he worked with a single-minded determination.

Dane grabbed hold of a chunk of bricks and

mortar the size of a scuba tank, and heaved. Cool air blew across his face, and his light shone into an open passageway.

"I think we did it!"

"Hell yes!" Bones exclaimed. "But if we come across another blockage, I'm going to need a couple of beers before we get to work."

Laughing with relief, they cleared a hole large enough to worm their way through, and soon found themselves back in the passageway they'd followed into Faneuil Hall. That had been only hours ago, but it seemed like days, weeks even.

They reached the exit at the base of Paul Revere's statue and paused.

"It's the middle of the day on the Fourth of July. What are people going to think when we climb out of here?"

"You know what, Maddock? I don't care."

They pushed the cover aside and Bones gave Dane a leg up. Blinded by daylight after so many hours in the dark, he squeezed his eyes closed against the glare, and opened them to find himself surrounded by a crowd of men, women, and children, all decked out in star spangled attire and gaping at him.

"City inspectors. Checking out some problems with the sewer system." Dane reached down, grabbed Bones' hand, and hauled him up.

"You folks enjoy your holiday," Bones added. "And remember us poor suckers who don't get a day off on the Fourth. Gotta love Uncle Sam." He winked at a leggy blonde who giggled and blushed.

The crowd broke apart as Dane replaced the trail marker. When he stood and turned around, Bones was chatting up the blonde, who had been joined by her friend, a curvy brunette with big, brown eyes.

"Maddock, this is Courtney and her friend Melissa. I think we should blow off work and hang out with them."

Dane managed a nod, transfixed by Melissa, the brunette. He'd never seen eyes so beautiful. "Yeah, how about Bones and I get cleaned up and we'll meet up in a couple of hours?"

"Where should we meet?" Courtney asked.

"How about that bar where they film *Cheers*?" Bones asked. "I've always liked Sam. That dude is a player."

"The Bull and Finch?" Melissa said. "You know they don't actually film..."

Dane cut her off with a wave of his hand. "Don't bother," he whispered as Bones and Courtney debated the merits of Coach versus Woody. "He'll pretend he doesn't know what you're talking about. He's not dumb, but he'll drive you nuts pretending he is."

"You two make an odd pair." Melissa looked him up and down, but Dane kept his eyes locked on hers. How did she manage to hold his gaze like that? "Of course, so do Courtney and I." She lowered her voice, "Unfortunately, she *is* as dumb as she acts, but she's sweet."

"I wouldn't call Bones 'sweet,' but he's all right."

"Sometimes, the Yin and Yang friendships are the ones that last." Melissa took his hand and held it up, frowning at the black dirt beneath his fingernails. "You've got a seriously dirty job. I'd find a new line of work if I were you."

"Actually, that was just a cover story so people wouldn't wonder why we were down in the tunnels."

"Really? This sounds interesting."

"It is, but it'll take a long time to explain." He glanced over her shoulder to see Bones fix him with a disapproving look. "Actually, it won't take that long. We're history junkies and we heard there were old tunnels under the city that dated back to Colonial times. We decided to check it out and the ceiling fell in."

Melissa laughed. "I can see why you'd want to make up a cover story." She checked her watch. "We'll meet you in two hours. And don't you dare stand me up."

"Wouldn't dream of it."

As they made their way back to the spot where they'd left Andrews' car, they discussed their options.

"What do we do?" Bones asked. "I mean, do we report what happened?"

Dane considered the question. His first instinct was, and had always been, to trust in the truth. In this case, however, he couldn't see any way that telling the truth would accomplish anything other than complicating their lives. He sighed.

"I think we should forget the headquarters even exists. There's nothing left of it anyway, and if it were excavated, we'd have to explain two dead bodies."

"So the plan is?"

"We run Andrews' car through a carwash, take it back to his house, put it in the garage, and wipe it down for fingerprints, just to be on the safe side. Of course, as far as anyone knows, his death was an accident, so it's not like there'll be an investigation."

"And Jillian?"

"The crazy cat lady who never puts down roots? She skipped out on her lease and moved a little earlier than expected. She doesn't have any relatives who'll come looking for her. I suppose the Sons of the Republic might miss her."

"But they'll figure she's just another victim of their twisted game of King of the Mountain." Bones clapped a hand on Dane's shoulder. "I think you've got all the bases covered. Maddock, I am definitely rubbing off on you."

CHAPTER 19

"The prodigal sons have returned, and in one piece, I'm glad to see." It was a relief to find him so relaxed after their encounter a few days earlier. "You two didn't try to kill each other?"

"Actually, we got along okay. Much to my surprise."

"He's got a long way to go yet, but I'll get Maddock straightened out for you," Bones added.

"You didn't get him into any shenanigans, did you, Bonebrake?"

"I can honestly say *I* didn't get *him* into any trouble." Bones covered a laugh, but Maxie, his attention diverted by the morning paper, didn't notice. "We downed a few brews, he dragged me to some historical crap, I scammed on the ladies and Maddock took notes. The usual."

Chuckling, Maxie closed his newspaper and dropped it on the desk. "I read about a tunnel collapse yesterday in downtown Boston. Formed a big sinkhole in an abandoned lot. You didn't see that, did you?"

Dane and Bones spoke over each other in their hurry to reply.

"No."

"We didn't do it."

Maxie's features froze in a blank stare. They stood there in silence for a span of ten heartbeats, waiting to see what he would say next. Finally, his shoulders sagged and he dropped his chin to his chest. When he looked up again, Dane saw fatigue and a touch of amusement in his eyes.

"Do I need to make some calls?"

"I don't think so." Dane couldn't quite meet Maxie's eye.

"Good." Maxie returned to his newspaper and flipped to the sports page. He studied it for a minute, leaving Dane and Bones standing there. Dane was just about to ask if they were dismissed when Maxie spoke from behind the paper.

"Remember the questions I asked you both?"

"Which ones?" Bones asked.

"Tell me about Maddock."

"He's still got a stick up his butt, but it's smaller." Bones cleared his throat. "And his instincts are good. He's somebody you can trust."

"Maddock, tell me about Bonebrake."

"He's a little reckless, but he's tough and loyal. He'd run through a brick wall to help a friend."

"Or tear one down," Bones added with a grin.

Maxie gave them another long look. "It's a start. I'll make SEALs of you two yet. Dismissed."

Dane had his hand on the doorknob when Maxie called out.

"By the way, Maddock."

Dane froze and slowly turned his head toward Maxie. "Yes?"

"Paccone's an ass. Nice work."

Bones guffawed and shoved a dumbstruck Dane out the door and into the warm California sun.

"That," Bones proclaimed, "calls for a beer. How about I stand you to a pitcher?"

"Only if you let me buy the second one."

"It's a deal." Bones paused and gazed thoughtfully up at the sky.

"What?" Dane craned his neck to see what had captured Bones' attention, but saw only blue sky.

"I was just wondering. Do you think we'll ever have another adventure like that one?"

"Not a chance, my friend. Not a chance."

~The End~

About the Authors

David Wood is the author of The Dane Maddock Adventures series, as well as several stand-alone works and two series for young adults. Under his David Debord pen name he is the author of the Absent Gods fantasy series. He co-hosts the ThrillerCast podcast and is a contributing author at Thriller Central. When not writing, he coaches fast-pitch softball and tries to find time to read. David and his family live in Santa Fe, New Mexico. Visit him online at www.davidwoodweb.com.

Sean Sweeney's love of reading began in 1988, when he was handed J.R.R. Tolkien's classic The Hobbit, and was given a needed reading boost with John Grisham novels and the Star Wars Expanded Universe in the 1990s. His passion for writing began in 1993, as a sophomore in high school, when he began writing sports for his local newspaper. Sweeney has written for several newspapers and radio stations. Since then, Sean has written fifteen novels along with a handful of novellas and short stories. Sean lives in Bolton, Massachusetts with his girlfriend, Jennifer, their three horses, five cats, a bunny, and the betta fish that makes Sean's office its home.

Enjoy this sneak preview of

ATLANTIS

Sofia Perez mopped her brow and looked out a across the sun-baked flats of the Marisma de Hinojos. Heat rose in waves off from the parched earth, shimmering in the summer sun. Workers milled about, excavating the circles of canals that ringed the site. It was hard to believe the transformation this drought-ridden salt marsh outside of Cadiz, Spain had undergone since they'd begun work in the early spring. With the kind of funding they were getting, they'd better make progress.

"Hot as Satan's buttcrack out here." Patrick fanned himself with his straw pith helmet. His fair skin was not holding up well under the Spanish sun. In fact, his entire body glowed red beneath a thick layer of sunscreen. "I don't know how you handle it."

"I'm from Miami. This is nothing." That wasn't entirely true. She kept going to her backpack for the can of spray-on sports sunblock to protect her olive skin. She hated sunburns. She raised an eyebrow at Patrick. "So, are you going to stand there trying not to smile, or are you going to tell me what's up?"

"You're needed at my dig site." He stopped fanning. "We think we've found the entrance to the temple."

Now it was Sofia's turn to keep her emotions in check.

"No vendas la piel del oso antes de cazarlo," she said under her breath.

"What's that, now?"

"Something my abuela used to say. It means, *don't sell the bearskin before you hunt it.*" Now she did permit herself a sad smile. Her grandparents had been so proud when she'd graduated from college. They weren't as impressed by her choice of archaeology as a vocation. They'd been praying for an attorney in the family.

"It's more colorful than, *don't count your chickens before they hatch*, I'll grant you that. Now, are you coming?"

They navigated the busy work site, waving to workers who called out greetings to them. Spirits were high. This had been a controversial undertaking from the start. Sofia had been skeptical, but the money was too good to pass up. Since then, their results continued to vindicate them. The circles originally spotted in satellite imagery and scoffed at by almost everyone had proved, upon excavation, to be ringed canals. And at the center...

"The Temple of Poseidon," Patrick whispered. "I can't believe we've really found it. It's almost like a dream."

"You're a scientist, Patrick. Be professional."

"Even if it's not what we think, it's still a spectacular find. The architecture is classic, the golden ratio is everywhere. We uncovered a shaft that runs down into the temple at precisely the same angle as one of the shafts in the Queen's Chamber of the Great

Pyramid, except it's much bigger. A few inches wider and I'd have climbed down there myself. It's a great find, Sofia. We're going to be in the history books."

"We can't draw any conclusions until we get inside and see what, exactly we're dealing with. It would be pretty embarrassing if we told the world we've found the legendary temple at the heart of Atlantis and it turns out to be a grain storage building."

Patrick looked away, a guilty expression on his face.

Sofia stopped in her tracks, grabbed him by the shoulder, and yanked him around to face her. "Tell me you didn't." But the look in his eyes said that he had.

"I only sent one text. I was supposed to report in if we found anything promising. You've got to admit this," he pointed to the peak of the roof they had uncovered, "is interesting."

She couldn't argue with him. The temple, for it was clear that's what it was, had been remarkably well preserved. The carving on the pediment, the triangular upper portion of the temple facade, showed an angry Poseidon slamming his trident into the sea, sending ferocious waves in either direction. They'd uncovered only the two center supporting columns so far, massive pillars fluted with parallel, concave grooves. At their peaks, the capitals, the head pieces that flared out to support the horizontal beam beneath the pediment, were carved to resemble the scaled talons of a sea creature, giving the impression that the roof was in the clutches of a primordial beast. The sight of it sent chills down her spine.

"Who did you tell?"

"Mister Bishop. I mean, his assistant. That's the only number I had. They're staying somewhere nearby." His voice took on a pleading tone. "Come on, Sofia. They're footing the bill for this entire dig. They've given us everything we could want. You think we could have written grants to find Atlantis in southern Spain and gotten anything but ridicule for our trouble?"

"I know." She hated to admit it, but he was right. "It's just weird that the Kingdom Church is paying us to find Atlantis. Noah's Ark, I could see, but this? It's weird."

"I don't care as long as the checks keep coming. Now, how about you quit worrying and let's get down there so they can open this door. You said not to open anything without you, and we took you at your word."

"Good." A forty foot ladder descended into the pit where the excavation was ongoing. She climbed down, almost losing her footing once as she wondered what they would find inside.

Several people were gathered around the entrance to the temple. They had cleared the entire front of the temple and back through the pronaos, the covered area that led back to the naos, the temple's enclosed central structure, and now waited for her to give the word. She could almost fee their excitement as she mounted the steps and approached the doorway. This was the moment!

"The door is weird," Patrick said. "It's not really a door at all. It's more like a patch."

She didn't need to ask him to explain. The exposed portion of the naos was solid marble. The entryway, by contrast, looked like it had been sealed with loose stones and mortar.

"Looks like they wanted to keep something out," she said. "Maybe they knew the flood was coming?"

"Or they wanted to keep something in." Patrick made a frightened face, eliciting a giggle from a plump, female grad student.

"Clear it out. Try to keep it on one piece, if you can. And be careful."

The crew didn't need to be told twice. Clearly, this is what they'd been eager to do since uncovering the entryway. They worked with an efficiency that made her proud and, sooner that she would have thought possible, they worked the plug free.

"Ladies first." Patrick made a mocking bow and motioned for her to enter the temple.

Sofia paused on the ambulatory and took a deep breath. Was she about to make one of the greatest archaeological finds of all time? Heart racing, she fumbled with her flashlight, turned it on, and shakily directed the beam inside.

The cella, the interior chamber, hadn't been completely impervious to the disaster that befell the city. A foot-deep layer of silt covered the floor, and signs of leakage were all about, but it could have been worse. Much worse. This place had been sealed up tight and must have been covered by dirt and sand fairly quickly, at least by geological standards, to have kept it in such pristine condition. Mother Earth had wrapped it in her protective blanket, protecting it against the ravages of time.

She played her light around the room, and what she saw took her breath away. Twin colonnades, the columns shaped like the twisting tentacles of a sea serpent, ran the length of the room, framing a magnificent sight.

"What do you see?" Patrick had hung back, like he knew he was supposed to, but his anxious tone indicated he wouldn't wait much longer.

"Poseidon!" A twenty-foot tall statue of the Greek god stood atop a dais in the middle of the temple. Like the image on the pediment outside, this was an angry god, driving furious waves before him. Unlike so many modern interpretations, he was not a wise, grandfatherly figure, gray of hair and beard, but young and virile, with black hair and sinuous muscles. Wait... black hair?

"You can still see some of the paint!" she exclaimed. Through the use of ultraviolet light, researchers had determined that the Greeks had actually painted over their sculptures, sometimes in bright primary colors, other times in more subdued, natural tones. This sculpture appeared to have been done in the latter style. Besides the traces of black in the hair, she could see hints of bronze skin and flecks of silver on his trident, and the waves beneath his feet were coated in aqua tones with streaks of white at the crests of the waves. Had leaks in the roof eroded the paint, or had the pigments merely faded over time?

One of the many questions they would doubtless try to answer as they studied this fabulous place. She

Her crew could wait no longer, but crowded in behind her, adding their own flashlight beams to the scant light hers provided.

"Whoa." Patrick, focused on the Poseidon statue, stumbled on the soft, uneven dirt. "It's just..." Words failed him, so he shook his head, continuing to gaze at the sculpture of the god of the sea.

"What's the Stonehenge thing?" The girl who had laughed at Patrick indicated a circle of altars that ringed the statue. Though they were marble, and their lines sharp, the thick bases and circular arrangement did suggest Stonehenge in miniature.

"And there's an obelisk where the heel stone should be." Patrick rounded the statue, kicking up a cloud of dust as he went. "Hey, wait a minute." He froze. "Sofia?"

"What is it?" She joined him on the far side of the statue and immediately saw what had stopped him in his tracks. The back wall that divided the cella from the adyton, the area to which only priests were admitted, sloped away from them, and each layer of stone grew progressively smaller, giving the illusion of...

"A pyramid," Patrick whispered.

"Why not? We've got an obelisk here. Perhaps Atlantis was, in some way, a cultural forerunner to the Greeks and the Egyptians." She wanted to kick herself. Such speculation was unscientific and unprofessional. She turned the beam of her flashlight into the adyton and almost dropped it.

The light gleamed on a contraption of silver metal supported on four stone pillars. It was a pyramid-shaped frame made of a metal that looked like Titanium. Suspended beneath it was a metal bowl shaped like a satellite dish. The pyramid was capped by a grasping silver hand. Only the hieroglyphs running around the cap just below the hand looked like something from the ancient world. Otherwise, its appearance was thoroughly modern…

…and thoroughly alien.

ATLANTIS
A Dane Maddock Adventure
Coming Summer, 2013!

Made in the USA
Lexington, KY
02 March 2014